THE SINS OF THE CITIES OF THE PLAIN

THE SINS OF THE CITIES OF THE PLAIN

EDITED WITH AN INTRODUCTION BY

WOLFRAM SETZ

VALANCOURT BOOKS

The Sins of the Cities of the Plain
Originally privately printed, London, 1881
First Valancourt Books edition 2012, reprinted 2014

ISBN 978-1-934555-31-6

Published by Valancourt Books
Richmond, Virginia
http://www.valancourtbooks.com

INTRODUCTION

Some years ago, Neil Bartlett devoted his search for clues to Oscar Wilde (*Who Was That Man?*), among others, to "Jack Saul of Lisle Street" and quoted thereby the words with which Jack Saul introduced himself in *The Sins of the Cities of the Plain* (p. 5): "Saul, Jack Saul, sir, of Lisle Street, Leicester Square, and ready for a lark with a free gentleman at any time."[1] The connection of the name Jack Saul with Oscar Wilde is not arbitrary: we know that Oscar Wilde read *The Sins of the Cities of the Plain*. This information is part of the history of the novel *Teleny*, which until today is above all connected primarily with the name of Oscar Wilde. Charles Hirsch, who came in 1889 from Paris to London and soon took over the Librairie Parisienne, reported in the preface to the French edition of *Teleny* that Oscar Wilde bought from him not only "novels by the best authors: Zola, Maupassant, Bourget, etc.", but also "certain licentious works, of a special kind, designated by the euphemism of 'socratic'". One of these books was *The Sins of the Cities of the Plain*.[2]

Perhaps one may also detect in *Teleny* a literary response to Jack Saul's "factual report": the city of Sodom is repeatedly directly named, but beside it Sodom and Gomorrah are mentioned with the description "Cities of the Plain"—and with a clearly positive emphasis: The "sins

1 Neil Bartlett, *Who Was That Man? A Present for Mr Oscar Wilde* (London: Serpent's Tail, 1988), p. xv.

2 Charles Hirsch's "Notice bibliographique" (English translation), in *Teleny, or, The Reverse of the Medal. A Physiological Romance of To-Day, attributed to Oscar Wilde and others*. Edited with an introduction and notes by Amanda Mordavsky Caleb (Kansas City: Valancourt Books, 2010), pp. 171-175, quotation pp. 171-172.

of the Cities of the Plain" became the "pleasures of the
Cities of the Plain": " 'Ah!' said the Spahi, quietly lighting a
cigarette, 'what pleasures can be compared with those of
the Cities of the Plain?' "[1] The opening scene in *The Sins of
the Cities of the Plain* also seems to have its echo in *Teleny*.
In the search for Teleny and Briancourt, Des Grieux
meets various figures that force upon him the question of
"whether the cities of the plain had been destroyed by fire
and brimstone". And it is said of one of these men: "He
. . . walked on, then turned round on his heels, and stared
at me. . . . He lingered once more, let me pass, walked
on at a brisker pace, and was again beside me. Finally, I
looked at him. Though it was cold, he was but slightly
dressed. He wore a short, black velvet jacket and a pair
of light gray, closely-fitting trousers marking the shape of
the thighs and buttocks like tights."[2]

More important is the relationship between the two
works that results from a historical review. In nineteenth-
century England there was a series of scandals and trials
which were about homosexuality; the Wilde trials were
only the culmination. A quarter century earlier a similar
sensation was aroused by the trial of Boulton and Park,
which is directly addressed by Jack Saul in *The Sins of the
Cities of the Plain*: "You remember the Boulton and Park
case? Well, I was present at the ball given at Haxell's Hotel
in the Strand" (p. 38). The evening on which Boulton and
Park were arrested can be named: Thursday, 28 April 1870.
We even know what Stella (Ernest Boulton) and Fanny
(Frederick William Park) wore that evening and what collection of clothes they had.[3] In 1889, the Cleveland Street
scandal caused a stir, being concerned with the telegram
messengers in the service of Queen Victoria, who earned

1 *Teleny or The Reverse of the Medal* (2010), p. 132.
2 *Teleny or The Reverse of the Medal* (2010), pp. 86 and 84.
3 Bartlett, *Who Was That Man?*, pp. 131-133.

some extra money in a house in Cleveland Street. In the trial Jack (or John) Saul is one of the most important witnesses, "by then in his late thirties" and "still a professional 'Mary-Anne'".[1] The echo of this trial can still be heard in the Wilde trials: Wilde's novel *Dorian Gray* had been called a piece of literature for "outlawed noblemen and perverted telegraph boys" in a review,[2] and in the first Wilde trial passages of *Dorian Gray* were read aloud and evaluated as an indication of the immoral behavior of the author.[3]

The three trials reflect not only the difference in legislation, but also the different approach to the law. Valid in the mid-19th century, still unchanged, was what the English Parliament decided in 1533: "the detestable and abominable Vice of Buggery" should be considered a felony and punished accordingly.[4] Felony, originally infidelity to the feudal lord, had lost its meaning over the centuries, but the threat against sodomy remained; felony became a synonym for sodomy: "a 'felony' meant sodomy and nothing else".[5] "Conspiracy to commit a felonious crime" was in

1 Colin Simpson, Lewis Chester, and David Leitch, *The Cleveland Street Affair* (Boston: Little, Brown, 1976), pp. 49 and 52; Bartlett, *Who Was That Man?*, p. 89.

2 Charles Whibley, in *The Scots Observer*, July 1890, cited by Bartlett, *Who Was That Man?*, p. 94. See also Oscar Wilde, *The Picture of Dorian Gray. Authoritative Texts, Backgrounds, Reviews and Reactions, Criticism.* Edited by Donald L. Lawler (New York: W. W. Norton & Company, 1988), p. 346.

3 H. Montgomery Hyde (ed.), *Oscar Wilde* (Famous Trials, vol. 7) (London: Penguin Books, 1962), pp. 109-115; Merlin Holland, *Irish Peacock & Scarlet Marques. The Real Trial of Oscar Wilde* (London & New York: Fourth Estate, 2003), pp. 94-102. See Richard Ellmann, *Oscar Wilde* (New York: Vintage Books, 1988), pp. 448-452 ("The Cross-Examination").

4 H. Montgomery Hyde, *The Other Love: An Historical and Contemporary Survey of Homosexuality in Britain* (London: Heinemann, 1970), pp. 39 and 92.

5 Rupert Croft-Cooke, *Feasting with Panthers: A New Consideration of Some Late Victorian Writers* (London: W. H. Allen, 1967), pp. 49 and 54.

1870 the charge against Boulton and Park, but the penalty had changed: since 1861 sodomy was no longer threatened by the death penalty, but "only" life imprisonment (for attempted sodomy, imprisonment up to ten years). The restriction to the fact of anal intercourse (where it played in the formulation of 1533 no matter whether the act was "with mankind or beast") made detection difficult. Thus the doctor who was consulted in the case of Boulton and Park did not know how he was to provide such proof. He was not yet acquainted with the book (also quoted in *The Sins of the Cities of the Plain*) by the French physician Ambroise Tardieu, who since 1857 had described in ever new and expanded editions the "Crimes Against Public Morals" (*Étude medico-légale sur les attentats aux mœurs*). For him, undeniable evidence of active or passive pederasty was, respectively, "a very thin, dog-like penis" or "a funnel-shaped anus".[1] But even in his appearance the pederast was easy for him to recognize: "Curled hair, made-up skin, open collar, waist tucked in to highlight the figure, fingers, ears, chest loaded with jewelry, the whole body exuding an odor of the most penetrating perfumes, and in the hand a handkerchief, flowers, or some needlework: such is the strange, revolting and rightfully suspect physiognomy of the pederast."[2]

The trial had a good outcome for Boulton and Park; the charges were dropped. The court agreed with the strategy of the defense to hold everything as a joke. The two had not been surprised in a sexual act, but rather were arrested in a hotel where they had taken part as ladies at

1 See Angus McLaren, *Twentieth-Century Sexuality: A History* (Oxford: Blackwell, 1999), p. 91.
2 Vernon A. Rosario, *Inversion's Histories/History's Inversions: Novelizing Fin-de-Siècle Homosexuality*, in Vernon A. Rosario (ed.), *Science and Homosexualities* (New York & London: Routledge, 1997), pp. 89-107, quotation pp. 90-91.

a ball. Sodomy shuns the light of day, the defense had stated, it was associated with shame, is done secretly, and above all is an ugly thing. Quite different was the appearance of Boulton and Park, alias Stella and Fanny, who had showed themselves in their feminine costumes in public, without any shame and in the most audacious elegance. How could they be brought into connection with such offenses? The court agreed.[1]

What Jack Saul relates in *The Sins of the Cities of the Plain* about Boulton and Park seems like an ironic comment on the trial. Here it is reported as it actually had "been", here is described what the court did not wish to believe. The sexual directness had already been predetermined in a limerick that appeared in 1879 in the journal *Pearl*:

> There was an old person of Sark
> Who buggered a pig in the dark;
> The swine, in surprise,
> Murmured: "God blast your eyes,
> Do you take me for Boulton or Park?"[2]

The reality was not inferior to what is described in *The Sins of the Cities of the Plain*. The police records report the appearance of the collection of Fanny and Stella, and even quantify the estimated value of individual garments. Stella, we learn, at times as Mrs. Graham rented a coach and visited, with Fanny, theaters and restaurants, and even the famous boat races at Oxford and Cambridge. The driver said he would never have thought the two could not be women.[3] And if Stella had cards imprinted with "Lady

1 Bartlett, *Who Was That Man?*, pp. 141-142.
2 *The Pearl. A Journal of Facetiae and Voluptuous Reading*, No. 1, July 1879 (New York: Grove Press, 1968, p. 35); cited by Bartlett, *Who Was That Man?*, p. 102.
3 Croft-Cooke, *Feasting with Panthers*, p. 48.

Arthur Clinton", it was not a product of her fancy, but rather he/she was the lover of Lord Arthur Clinton. Her frivolous-teasing love letters were among the "evidence" in the trial. For Lord Clinton the scandal was anything but a joke: he withdrew from the trial by suicide. In *The Sins of the Cities of the Plain*, he appears again as "Lord Arthur".[1]

That Fanny and Stella did not constitute a unique case is confirmed by reports that Karl Heinrich Ulrichs had received in 1868 from London and included in his *Forschungen über das Räthsel der mannmännlichen Liebe* (*The Riddle of "Man-Manly" Love*): "In Paris and London there are flocks of beautiful young womanly types who wander about and flirt on the boulevards and sidewalks. This is also well known to the public there. In London, the people call them 'Mary Anns'." Ulrichs quotes from a newspaper report that, like Boulton and Park in 1871, three years previously two other "Urnings" appeared in court, one of whom, named Henry Maltravers, used the "maiden name" "Kate Smith". Sergeant Shillingford described the two as "being then painted and powdered, and difficult to tell, whether they were males or females". Ulrichs' London informant was involved in a close circle of "Urninge" and could thus also report on social events, including, among others, a report of an "Urning soirée", given by "Viola", "a young English Urning from a distinguished circle": "Of the twenty persons attending, four were brilliantly dressed as ladies. You would have sworn that a true woman was standing in front of you. The first appeared in poppy-red velvet with a long satin train, the second in black watered silk, the third in white silk trimmed with green lace, the fourth in bright pink and white satin. . . . One of them even wore real diamonds." Like the parties in the club of "Mr. Inslip" in *The*

---

1 See Morris B. Kaplan, *Sodom on the Thames: Sex, Love, and Scandal in Wilde Times* (Ithaca: Cornell University Press, 2005), pp. 51-62: "Portrait of a Marriage".

Sins of the Cities of the Plain, this soirée began very late: "The invitation was for twelve o'clock midnight, dinner was served at one o'clock, with dancing until seven o'clock in the morning."[1]

Pornographic literature as a mirror of the time—this also applies to other aspects of same-sex sexuality in *The Sins of the Cities of the Plain*. Fred Jones introduces us to the phenomenon of soldiers' prostitution ("'We all do it' said Fred to me . . . 'It's the commonest thing possible in the Army'", p. 33), which was by no means confined to England. Turned into something positive, the phenomenon of "soldier love" is praised by Karl Heinrich Ulrichs in his poem "Lieber ist mir ein Bursch . . ." ("Dearer to me is the lad village-born . . ."). John A. Symonds was so taken by this poem that he inserted a translation in his book on Walt Whitman: ". . . Dearest of all are the young, steel-thewed, magnificent soldiers— / Be it the massive form of a black-browed insolent guardsman, / Or a blue-eyed hussar with the down new-fledged on his firm lip— . . ."[2]

Typical for England is the sex in the public schools. Such experiences are an integral part of a sexual initiation in the pornographic literature; Jack Saul experiences his first orgasm at the age of 10 years in a "boarding-school at Colchester" (p. 12). Already in 1810 the public schools were denounced as "a system of premature debauchery", and John A. Symonds observed in his school "obscene orgies of naked boys in bed together".[3] Alfred Douglas confessed

---

1 Karl Heinrich Ulrichs, *Memnon. Die Geschlechtsnatur des mannliebenden Urnings* (1868). English translation by Michael A. Lombardi-Nash: *The Riddle of 'Man-Manly' Love* (Buffalo, N.Y.: Prometheus Books, 1994), vol. 1, p. 307 and vol. 2, pp. 391-392.

2 See Hubert Kennedy, *Karl Heinrich Ulrichs: Pioneer of the Modern Gay Movement*. 2nd ed. (Concord, Calif.: Peremptory Publications, 2005), p. 57.

3 Louis Crompton, *Byron and Greek Love: Homophobia in 19th-Century England* (London: Faber and Faber, 1985), pp. 79-80.

in his relationship with Oscar Wilde only: "Oscar Wilde's aberrations were simply and exactly what might be described as 'the usual public schoolboy business', neither more nor less."[1]

By 1886 the legal situation was decisively changed. In order to curb prostitution, it was more strongly criminalized, and at the last minute, a provision was added to the new law, that all homosexual acts, even in the private sector, were to be penalized. The driving force was the MP Henry Labouchere, who, as editor of the weekly *Truth* exercised a great influence. The difficult-to-prove act of "sodomy" became, in the new law, the vague offense of "gross indecency". Blackmail of homosexuals in England was now an everyday crime. Of this law, which remained in force until 1967, even one of the lawyers involved in the Wilde trials, Travers Humphreys, had, on review, a strong criticism: "It is doubtful whether the House fully appreciated that the words 'in public or private' in the new clause had completely altered the law."[2]

The legal starting point was the same in the trial of the brothel in Cleveland Street in 1889 and the trials of Oscar Wilde. What was different was the handling of the law. In 1889, the procedure was altogether hesitant; those condemned were only a few of the older telegram messengers who had recruited their younger colleagues for the brothel. The operator of the brothel was able to leave the country, as did Lord Arthur Somerset, a respected officer of Her Majesty, whom the boys identified as one of the guests. An arrest warrant was adopted only after he had turned his back on England. There was a special reason for this indulgence: rumor had it, that Prince Albert Victor ("Eddy"), son of the Prince of Wales, had been a

1 Lord Alfred Douglas, *Oscar Wilde: A Summing-up* (London: The Richards Press, 1940), p. 39.
2 *Oscar Wilde* (Famous Trials, 1962), p. 12.

guest in Cleveland Street. In Parliament, Labouchere complained that the new law had not been rigorously enough enforced and the police had been too lenient. At least in this point the witness Jack Saul agreed with him. We learn from the interrogation, not only details about the guests in the brothel, but also something of his changed circumstances. The brilliant times of *The Sins of the Cities of the Plain* were over. He complained that the telegram messengers, who indeed had a good job, were able to add to their earnings in the brothel, while he had to take to the streets. We learn further that he lived together with "Queen Anne", whose real name was Andrew Grant. On the astonished question, "And you were hunted out by the police?", he said, "No, they have never interfered. They have always been kind to me." And the question, "Do you mean they have deliberately shut their eyes to your infamous practices?", was answered with: "They have had to shut their eyes to more than me."[1]

Jack Saul was not prosecuted, the court, so to speak, not wanting to get their hands dirty. It was entirely different then in the trials of Oscar Wilde. At the end the judge spoke of the "worst case I have ever tried". For him Oscar Wilde was "the centre of a circle of extensive corruption of the most hideous kind among young men". He pronounced "the severest sentence that the law allows". In his judgment this sentence was "totally inadequate for such a case as this".[2]

In general, the Jack (or John) Saul of the trial of 1889/90 is identified with the Jack Saul of *The Sins of the Cities of*

1 Simpson, Chester, and Leitch, *The Cleveland Street Affair*, p. 156; Theo Aronson, *Prince Eddy and the Homosexual Underworld* (London: John Murray, 1994), p. 158.
2 *Oscar Wilde* (Famous Trials, 1962), p. 272; Ellmann, *Oscar Wilde*, p. 477.

the Plain. But the book is not a factual report. In the case of
the Jack Saul of the "Recollections" we have a fiction similar to that of Boulton and Park, who become here Jack
Saul's "colleague ladies" and friends. Literary fiction is
used in the book as a conscious play. A reader of the scene,
where Jack observes through a keyhole Boulton (Laura)
and Lord Arthur, is no sooner reminded of a similar scene
from John Cleland's *Fanny Hill*, than this is pointed out: "It
put me in mind of the scene between two youths which
Fanny Hill relates to have seen through a peephole at a
roadside inn" (p. 38). Just as Boulton and Park had to give
their names, the (unknown) author of *The Sins of the Cities
of the Plain* may have consciously given his protagonist the
name "Jack Saul".

The indirect account of the reports of others is also
to be evaluated as a literary stratagem: "Young Wilson"
and "George Brown" contribute their experiences to help
make more colorful the palette of reports on "sodomite"
doings in London. "Mr. Cambon", who at the beginning of
the book so readily reveals his name, may also be a literary
fiction. From him (or from the one for whom he stands)
comes perhaps the final chapter, which gathers all kinds
of (literary) gossip on the subject. As a possible author of
The Sins of the Cities of the Plain, James Campbell Reddie
has been brought into the discussion. His friend, the erotica collector Henry Spencer Ashbee, said that probably
no obscene book was unknown to him, no matter what
language it was written in. In addition, Reddie himself
had written erotic books: *The Amatory Experiences of a
Surgeon*, and probably also *The Adventures of a School-Boy,
or The Freaks of Youthful Passion*. In a short text entitled
Memoranda from Mr. P—, which appeared in November
1880 in the magazine *Pearl*,[1] right at the beginning a "Mr.

---

1   *The Pearl*, No. 17, Nov. 1880 (1968, pp. 598-602).

Reddie" is named. Patrick J. Kearney suspects that James Campbell Reddie, who died in 1878, could be meant. Since homosexuality is also a theme in all the texts mentioned, it seems reasonable to him to suspect that Reddie is also the author of *The Sins of the Cities of the Plain*.[1] The specific time references to the year 1881 in the appendix of the book ("Just as this is going to press there is a case in the London *Daily Telegraph* of July 9, 1881 . . .", p. 82) cannot thus be explained however: Even James Campbell Reddie, like Jack Saul, would need a "co-author".

The reference to the *Daily Telegraph* of July 9, 1881, is only the most obvious example of a number of references to specific events and books. Neil Bartlett has published the newspaper article in his book. It shows that *The Sins of the Cities of the Plain* reproduced it quite precisely, though the names have been omitted: "Serious Charge. John Cameron alias Sutherland, a corporal in the 2nd Battalion of the Scots Guards, was charged with one Count Guido zu Lynar, Secretary to the German Embassy, with the commission of an atrocious offense, at a coffee-house situated in Lower Sloane Street, Chelsea, where the two accused were apprehended."[2]

In addition, examples of the erotic literature of the time are cited. Boulton sings a ballad to music by himself from the magazine *Pearl*: "Don't you remember sweet Alice, Ben Bolt" (p. 50).[3] George Brown not only flung the name of his Jewish pickup into the public of a res-

1 Patrick J. Kearney, *A History of Erotic Literature* (London: Parragon, 1982), pp. 109-112.
2 Bartlett, *Who Was That Man?*, p. 104.
3 The quotation is slightly changed from the original: "Oh, do you remember sweet Polly, Ben Bolt, / Sweet Polly with a cunt soft and brown" (*The Pearl*, No. 15, Sept. 1880 [1968, p. 534]). See Patrick J. Kearney, *The Private Case: An Annotated Bibliography of the Private Case Erotica Collection in the British (Museum) Library* (London: Jay Landesman, 1981), pp. 275-276, nos. 1410-1415.

taurant ("'Mr. Simeon Moses' I said, speaking as loudly as possible"), but even added a reference to the novel *The Romance of Lust*, which the man had given him to read: "Would you like a bobby to find that book on you?" (p. 65). The four-volume work, published in 1873-1876, had been assembled by the "world traveler" William S. Potter; it was otherwise quoted in the pornographic literature, *e.g.*, in the novel *Sub-Umbra, or Sport Among the She-Noodles*, which appeared in installments in the magazine *Pearl*.[1] An example is also mentioned from the wealth of literature on flagellation: *Birchen Bouquet*, a collection of flagellant scenes that had a new edition in 1881—the year in which *The Sins of the Cities of the Plain* appeared.[2]

The Appendix to *The Sins of the Cities of the Plain* (*The Same Old Story: Arses Preferred to Cunts—A Short Essay on Sodomy, etc.—Tribadism*) is of little interest: there are no comments on the legal situation in England, nothing on attempts to explain and justify "man-manly love". In the "essays" in *The Sins of the Cities of the Plain* the term "sodomy" varies between gender-unspecific anal sex and what one would name at the end of the century, in England too, with the term "homosexuality". As witnesses, Juvenal and Martial are called on, with their satires and epigrams, and Suetonius, with the gossip in his biographies of Roman emperors; for tribadism an anecdote from the memoirs of the Count de Grammont is quoted, which deals with "Miss Hobart, a maid of honour at the court of Charles the Second" (p. 88). Just as random appear witnesses from the present: the already mentioned Tardieu and an unspecified travel report ("interesting remarks published privately by a recent traveller through the realms of the King

1 *The Pearl*, No. 7, Jan. 1880 (1968, p. 218): ". . . the idea having been suggested to me by reading a book called *The Romance of Lust*."
2 Kearney, *The Private Case*, p. 115, no. 250.

of Bokhara", p. 85).[1] This is all garnished with speculation about the prevalence of homosexuality in England and elsewhere in the world.

*

The Sins of the Cities of the Plain is a pornographic text and also an important cultural and historical document. Thus, H. Montgomery Hyde, who already discussed the book in detail almost half a century ago in his *History of Pornography*, could take over his evaluation unchanged in his book *The Other Love*: "Although some of the details of the incidents described in *The Sins of the Cities of the Plain* may be exaggerated for effect, the work is based upon fact and no doubt gives a faithful enough picture of a seamy side of contemporary London life."[2] This view has been strengthened in the meantime by many authors; William A. Cohen, for example, in his book *Sex Scandal* speaks of "a peculiar mixture of programmatic pornographic narrative with apparently factual, and potentially exposing, information",[3] and Morris B. Kaplan speaks of "an epic of polymorphous pansexuality and gender fuck":

1 See Eduard Eversmann, *Reise von Orenburg nach Buchara* (Berlin: Christiani, 1823), pp. 83-84: "Gewiß in keinem Lande, selbst nicht in Constantinopel, ist Päderastie so im Schwunge als hier; . . . der chan selbst unterhält für sich in seiner Burg außer seinen Weibern, noch eine ganze Hetze (40 bis 60 Stück) Knaben, obgleich er dergleichen Verbrechen bei andern strenge bestraft." [Certainly in no land, not even in Constantinople, is pederasty so rampant as here; . . . even the Khan keeps for himself in his castle, in addition to his wives, a whole rabble of boys (40 to 60), although he strictly punishes others for the same crime.]

2 H. Montgomery Hyde, *A History of Pornography* (1964) (paperback edition, New York: Dell, 1966), p. 152; H. Montgomery Hyde, *The Other Love*, p. 123.

3 William A. Cohen, *Sex Scandal: The Private Parts of Victorian Fiction* (Durham: Duke University Press, 1996), p. 124.

"Most of these scenes cross boundaries defining gender roles and sexual propriety, age cohorts and social classes. Schoolmasters have sex with their pupils; employers with servants; customers with clerks; brothers with sisters; noble lords with rough lads; respectable bourgeois with drag queens. However fantasmatic the elaboration, the landscape is recognizably late Victorian London."[1]

"Finally back in print" promised the cover of a supposed new edition in 1992 with a slightly different title: Anonymous, *Sins of the Cities of the Plain*. Whoever trusted this text was, however, led astray, for it was not the text of 1881, but only "a seriously distorted modern edition" (Cohen). Paul Hallam was probably the first to warn against the "Badboy" text from the publisher "Masquerade Books". In his anthology *The Book of Sodom* (1993) he tells how he had years earlier in the British Library, under the strict supervision of a librarian, read in one of the few available original copies: "The language of old porn, an erotic relation with its characters' timeless deeds yet dated words, I always find it oddly moving." No wonder he became convinced that the book was "worthy of republication". Accordingly he was pleased when the text appeared to be easily available and at a reasonable price (the original edition "cost four guineas so you'd need to be a lord to afford it"). The disappointment was swift: "My suspicion was aroused when Saul's 'appendage' was compared to a 'tremendous length of sausage'. A disgraceful addition." His conclusion: "The linguistic and historical interest is confused by the Masquerade edition being precisely that—modern porn masquerading as 'a classic'."[2]

Already in the brief opening scene the Masquerade ghostwriter has incorporated sex. As the two protagonists

---

1 Kaplan, *Sodom on the Thames*, pp. 222-223.
2 Paul Hallam, *The Book of Sodom* (London & New York: Verso, 1993), pp. 17 and 19-20.

have not yet met, however, and besides find themselves in a public place, everything is at first played out in the imagination. The original text, too, is thoroughly concerned with what Saul's body promises: "That lump in his trousers had quite a fascinating effect upon me. Was it natural or made up by some artificial means? If real, what a size when excited; how I should like to handle such a manly jewel, etc." (p. 3). The Badboy version, however, does not leave it at the "etc.":

> "Why, I would run the palm of my hand down its great length, and binding it in my fingers I would surely pull at it until it began to thicken and rise before my eyes. Wetting it with spittle to facilitate further frigging, I would watch and grin as it gleamed and wriggled in my hand, slowly climbing its way to its full and remarkable height. Perhaps his breathtaking cock would need the two of my hands to frig it, as one would be too small to fit properly 'round its girth. Then two it would be, and I would pull at it up and down until his breathing became short and sharp. Then, without mercy or thought to elongating his pleasure, I would quicken my pace and set him aflame with anticipation for the coming explosion. Faster would I pull and tug o'er the grand length of this marvelous cock I had discovered, gleeful at the reddening of its head as it begins to drool and expands to its greatest proportions. Then, stammering under the intensity of my work, he would release himself to the heavens, and his swollen member would finally burst with boiling streams of creamy spendings. Jet after jet of it would rise and arc o'er his body, falling to splatter upon his chest and belly, flowing down into the nest of hair within the crook of his thighs."[1]

---

1 Anonymous, *Sins of the Cities of the Plain* (New York: Masquerade Books, 1992), pp. 8-9.

A second example of the enrichment of the text by pornographic scenes: In the original, in only a few sentences, we
read the following episode concerning a "junior teacher"
(p. 69):

> "There was one young fellow, who, being rather of
> a superior education to the rest, was made a junior
> teacher in the school. Well, do you know the boys of
> his class would actually frig him as he sat at his desk
> to hear their lessons, for the head schoolmaster was
> mostly asleep, and no one else dared say a word. This
> fairly broke his health down, and he had to go into the
> infirmary."

In the Badboy edition this is made into a separate plot (pp.
139-142). The assistant teacher gets the name Master Kent,
knows about the narrator's many sexual adventures, and
not without reason prefers to use the students' toilet instead of the toilet for teachers: "The other masters were
all quite old, curmudgeonly and crotchety, and really nothing to look at. Why bother taking a pee beside the likes of
them, when one can look on at the young flesh relieving
themselves in the boys' chambers." There he is surprised
one day by the narrator—in this part of the book, it is
not Jack Saul, but George Brown: "There peeping over the
partition which separated one sitting stall from the next,
was dear green-eyed young Master Kent, as he spied some
illicit activity going on within the next chamber!" There
follows, extended over several pages, an orgy with Will,
the "handsome young power-house of a boy". Then it's
back to the original text, but here the comment on the
disastrous consequences of the "frigging" ("this sordid
activity fairly broke his health down") becomes almost
grotesque.

Anyone who reads the Badboy text must necessarily
come to an incorrect assessment. Thus Byrne R. S. Fone

admits in his book *A Road to Stonewall*, that *The Sins of the Cities of the Plain* does offer "some information about male prostitution and the London locales in which it was practiced", but this information only served "to describe yet another massive organ, splendid endowment, athletic encounter". The original text could not have provided him with this impression; he had not read and evaluated the text of 1881, but rather the Badboy version of 1992. He quotes as an example the beginning of *The Sins of the Cities of the Plain*. The Badboy addition which compares the "male appendages" to a "tremendous length of sausage" he does leave out (indicated by three dots), but it is this and similar additions that determine his judgment.[1]

The Badboy text is characterized not only by "disgraceful additions" (Hallam). Even worse is a continuous distortion of the situations and details, and a linguistic "modernization" in the sense of political correctness. The continuous distortion has perhaps taken in Phillip Winn when he says: "Saul's sexual experiences . . . are almost exclusively male-to-male and adult in nature."[2] With this, again only the Badboy version is described. Here, in fact, all the episodes in which females are involved, are rewritten into a purely male situation. The episodes will thus not only have a different status; since the focus of the ghostwriter is more on the painting of the sex scenes than on the harmonization of the new text, curious things arise. Thus the six-year-old Jack at a family gathering stares at his 17-year-old cousin Jenny, because she has facial hair: "What have you got girl's clothes on for? I don't believe

---

1 Byrne R. S. Fone, *A Road to Stonewall. Male Homosexuality and Homophobia in English and American Literature, 1750-1969* (New York: Twayne Publishers, 1995), p. 117.

2 Phillip Winn, *Taxonomic trends, literary fashions and lace handkerchiefs: the decadent aesthete as homosexual in vogue.* In *Mots pluriels*, No. 10, April 1999 (http://motspluriels.arts.uwa.edu.au/MP1099pw.html).

you are a girl at all. My brother Dick has got a mustache just like yours." Called to order, he adds: "I know she's a boy. See if I don't find out whether she's cracked like a girl, or got a spout like a tea-kettle on her" (p. 11). This time he is sent from the room. Twelve years later, he meets Jenny again for the first time, and then they find their way to one another on a "friendly sofa". In 1992, Jenny has became Jerry, Jack is no longer six years old, but already "late in my teens" and "aware of my predilection". That the encounter there takes a completely different course is hardly surprising (pp. 28-35).

The original Jack says, "I met with an adventure with the other sex when I was nearly fourteen"; in the 1992 edition, he has to wait until he is "nearly eighteen". But then nothing at all comes of it, because Sarah, the "young dairymaid about eighteen, a fine dark-eyed wench, very good looking, a strapping big, strong young woman, with rare plump arms and splendid full bosom" of 1881 (p . 16), from one sentence to the next, becomes Klaus, "an elder farm servant of about fifty-two, a rugged and dark-eyed man of expansive and well-proportioned dimension" (p. 48). From Sarah, he has still retained only the "splendid full bosom".

The Jack of 1881—as mentioned—at 10 years old was sent to a "boarding-school at Colchester" (p. 12) and became acquainted with sex in the circle of boys. In 1992, the eighteen-year-old Jack goes to the "college at Gloucester" (p. 39), and although he has only a few pages earlier wildly carried on with Jerry, he too is also introduced into bedroom sex like a ten-year-old. . . .

Examples of such absurdities can be easily multiplied. That all younger persons, like Jack himself, are made older almost goes without saying, and political correctness also requires that "pederastic games" (p. 5) become harmless "clandestine games" and the "nigger" (p. 58) may only be a "black man".

In 2006 there appeared in the "Olympia Press" a further edition, in which Jack Saul is now named as author: Jack Saul, *Sins of the Cities of the Plain*.[1] This time, it explicitly states: "First Published 1881". But that's not true. "First published 1992" would be correct, because what follows is again not the original text, but almost unchanged the Badboy text. The newly revived Olympia Press does not honor its historical predecessor with it; the falsification threatens to become the original.[2] It is high time, 130 years after the publication of the original edition, to make the original text again available.[3]

WOLFRAM SETZ

---

1 Jack Saul, *Sins of the Cities of the Plain* (The Olympia Press. The New Traveller's Companion Series, No. 91, 2006), also available as an e-book.
2 See John de St. Jorre, *Venus Bound: The Erotic Voyage of the Olympia Press and its Writers* (New York: Random House, 1994).
3 The present edition is based on the two-volume original edition of 1881, a microfilm of which was graciously provided by the British Library (Signature: P. C. 14. h. 10). See Kearney, *The Private Case*, p. 315, no. 1718. There appears to have been in the same year a second edition in one volume; see Pisanus Fraxi, *Catena Librorum Tacendorum. Bio-Biblio-Icono-graphical and Critical Notes on Curious, Uncommon and Erotic Books* [1885] (New York: Jack Brussel, 1962), pp. 194-195. Another edition appeared in 1890: Kearney, *The Private Case*, p. 315, no. 1719.

THE SINS

OF THE

CITIES OF THE PLAIN

OR THE

RECOLLECTIONS OF A MARY-ANN

WITH SHORT ESSAYS ON

SODOMY AND TRIBADISM

▶—:o:—◀

IN TWO VOLUMES

▶—:o:—◀

VOLUME I.

LONDON

PRIVATELY PRINTED

1881

RECOLLECTIONS OF A MARY-ANN

INTRODUCTION

The writer of these notes was walking through Leicester Square one sunny afternoon last November, when his attention was particularly taken by an effeminate, but very good-looking young fellow, who was walking in front of him, looking in shop-windows from time to time, and now and then looking round as if to attract my attention.

Dressed in tight-fitting clothes, which set off his Adonis-like figure to the best advantage, especially about what snobs call the fork of his trousers, where evidently he was favoured by nature by a very extraordinary development of the male appendages; he had small and elegant feet, set off by pretty patent leather boots, a fresh looking beardless face, with almost feminine features, auburn hair, and sparkling blue eyes, which spoke as plainly as possible to my senses, and told me that the handsome youth must indeed be one of the "Mary-Ann's" of London, who I had heard were often to be seen sauntering in the neighbourhood of Regent Street, or the Haymarket, on fine afternoons or evenings.

Presently the object of my curiosity almost halted and stood facing the writer as he took off his hat, and wiped his face with a beautiful white silk handkerchief.

That lump in his trousers had quite a fascinating effect upon me. Was it natural or made up by some artificial means? If real, what a size when excited; how I should like to handle such a manly jewel, etc. All this ran through my mind, and determined me to make his acquaintance, in order to unravel the real and naked truth; also, if possible, to glean what I could of his antecedents and mode of life, which I felt sure must be extraordinarily interesting.

When he moved on again I noticed that he turned down a little side street, and was looking in a picture shop. I followed him, and first making some observations about the scanty drapery on some of the actresses and other beauties whose photographs were exposed for sale, I asked him if he would take a glass of wine.

He appeared to comprehend that there was business in my proposal, but seemed very diffident about drinking in any public place.

"Well," I said, "would you mind if we take a cab to my chambers—I live in the Cornwall Mansions, close to Baker Street Station—have a cigar and a chat with me, as I see you are evidently a fast young chap, and can put me up to a thing or two?"

"All right. Put your thing up, I suppose you mean. Why do you seem so afraid to say what you want?" he replied with a most meaning look.

"I'm not at all delicate; but wish to keep myself out of trouble. Who can tell who hears you out in the streets?" I said, hailing a cab. "I don't like to be seen speaking to a young fellow in the street. We shall be all right in my own rooms."

It was just about my dinner hour when we reached my place, so I rang the bell, and ordered my old housekeeper to lay the table for two, and both of us did ample justice to a good rumpsteak and oyster sauce, topped up with a couple of bottles of champagne of an extra sec brand.

As soon as the cloth was removed, we settled ourselves comfortably over the fire with brandy and cigars, for it was a sharp, frosty day out.

"My boy, I hope you enjoyed your dinner?" I said, mixing a couple of good warm glasses of brandy hot, "but you have not favoured me with your name. Mine you could have seen by the little plate on my door, is Mr. Cambon."

"Saul, Jack Saul, sir, of Lisle Street, Leicester Square, and ready for a lark with a free gentleman at any time. What was it made you take a fancy to me? Did you observe any particularly interesting points about your humble servant?" as he slyly looked down towards the prominent part I have previously mentioned.

"You seem a fine figure, and so evidently well hung that I had quite a fancy to satisfy my curiosity about it. Is it real or made up for show?" I asked.

"As real as my face, sir, and a great deal prettier. Did you ever see a finer tosser in your life?" he replied, opening his trousers and exposing a tremendous prick, which was already in a halfstanding state. "It's my only fortune, sir; but it really provides for all I want, and often introduces me to the best of society, ladies as well as gentlemen. There isn't a girl about Leicester Square but what would like to have me for her man, but I find it more to my interest not to waste my strength on women; the pederastic game pays so well, and is quite as enjoyable. I wouldn't have a woman unless well paid for it."

He was gently frigging himself as he spoke, and had a glorious stand by the time he had finished, so throwing the end of my cigar into the fire, I knelt down by his side to examine that fine plaything of his.

Opening his trousers more, I brought everything into full view—a priapus nearly ten inches long, very thick, and underhung by a most glorious pair of balls, which were surrounded and set off by quite a profusion of light auburn curls.

How I handled those appendages, the sack of which was drawn up so deliciously tight, which is a sure sign of strength, and that they have not been enervated by too excessive fucking or frigging. I hate to see balls hang loosely down, or even a fine prick with very small or scarcely any stones to it—these half-and-half tools are an abomination.

Gently frigging him, I tongued the ruby head for a minute or two, till he called out, "Hold, hold, sir, or you will get it in your mouth!"

This was not my game; I wanted to see him spend, so removing my lips, I pointed that splendid tool outwards over the hearthrug and frigged him quickly. Almost in a moment it came; first a single thick clot was ejected, like a stone from a volcano, then quite a jet of sperm went almost a yard high, and right into the fire, where it fizzled on the red-hot coals.

"By Jove, what a spend!" I exclaimed, "we will strip now, and have some better fun, Jack. I want to see you completely naked, my boy, as there is nothing so delightful as to see a fine young fellow when well formed and furnished in every respect. Will you suck me? That is what I like first; frigging you has only given me half a cockstand at present."

"You must be generous if I do, or you will not get me to come and see you here again," he answered with a smile, which had almost a girlish sweetness of expression.

We were soon stripped to the buff, and having locked the door, I sat down with my beautiful youth on my knee, we kissed each other, and he thrust his tongue most wantonly into my mouth, as my hands fairly travelled all over his body; but that glorious prick of his claimed most attention, and I soon had it again in a fine state of erection.

"Now kneel down and gamahuche me," I said, "whilst I can frig your lovely prick with my foot."

Seemingly to enter thoroughly into the spirit of the thing, he was on his knees in a moment, between my legs, and began to fondle my still rather limp pego most deliciously, taking the head fully into his voluptuously warm mouth, and rolling his tongue round the prepuce in the most lascivious manner it is possible to imagine.

I stiffened up at once under such exciting tittillations, which seemed to have a like effect upon his prick, which I could feel with my toes to be as hard as a rolling-pin, as my foot gently frigged and rolled it on his bended thigh, and he soon spent over my sole as it gently continued the exciting friction.

I now gave myself more and more to his gamahuching, now and then seizing his head with both hands, and raising his face to mine, we indulged in luscious love kisses, which prolonged my pleasure almost indefinitely. At last I allowed him to bring me to a crisis, and he swallowed every drop of my spendings with evident relish.

After resting awhile, and taking a little more stimulant, I asked him how he had come to acquire such a decided taste for gamahuching, to do it so deliciously as he did.

"That would be too long a tale to go into now," he replied. "Some other day, if you like to make it worth my while, I will give you the whole history."

"Could you write it out, or give me an outline so that I might put it into the shape of a tale?"

"Certainly; but it would take me so much time that you would have to make me a present of at least twenty pounds. It would take during three or four weeks several hours a day."

"I don't mind a fiver a week if you give me a fair lot, say thirty or forty pages of note-paper a week, tolerably well written," I replied.

And the arrangement was made for him to compile me "The Recollections of a Mary-Ann," which I suggested ought to be the title, although he seemed not at all to like the name as applied to himself, saying that that was what the low girls of his neighbourhood called him if they wished to insult him, however, he said at last, "the four fivers will make up for that."

"Now," he added, "I suppose you would like me to put it up for you, or rather into myself. But can you lend me such a thing as a birch? You are not so young as I am, and want something to stimulate you; besides, I want you to do it well, as I fancy that moderate sized cock of yours immensely. Do you know that I am sure I like a nice man to fuck me as much as ever a woman could?"

The birch was produced, and he insisted upon tying me down over the easy chair, so that I could not flinch or get away from the application of the rod.

He began very steadily, and with light stinging cuts which soon made me aware that I had a rather accomplished young schoolmaster to deal with my posteriors, which began to tingle most pleasantly after a few strokes. The sting of each cut was sharp, but the warm, burning rush of blood to the parts had such an exciting effect that, although I fairly writhed and wriggled under each stroke, I was rapidly getting into a most delicious state of excitement.

The light tips of the birch seemed to search out each tender spot, twining round my buttocks and thighs, touching up both shaft and balls, as well as wealing my ham, till I was most rampantly erect, and cried out for him to let me have him at once.

"Not yet; not yet, you bugger. You want to get into my arse, do you? I'll teach you to fuck arseholes, my boy!" he exclaimed, chuckling over my mingled pain and excitement.

"How do you like that—and that—and that—and that?" The last stroke was so painful that it almost took my breath away, and I knew he had fairly drawn blood.

I was furious, my prick felt red-hot, almost ready to burst, when he unloosed my hands and ancles.

I seized him in a perfect fury of lust. His prick was also standing like a bar of iron; he had got so excited by my flagellation. He was turned round, and made to kneel upon the chair at once, presenting his bottom to my attack. No one to look at it would have thought the pink and wrinkled little hole had ever been much used, except for the necessary offices of nature. The sight was perfectly maddening; it looked so delicious.

As I stopped for a moment to lubricate the head of my prick with saliva, he put his fingers in his mouth, and then wetted the little hole himself, to make it as easy as possible for me.

Coming to the charge, I found him delightfully tight, but I got in slowly as he helped me as much as possible by directing the head of my cock with his hand, whilst I had him round the waist and handled that beautiful tool of his, which added immensely to my pleasure. At last I felt fairly in, but did not want to spend too soon, so only moved very slowly, enjoying the sense of possession and the delicious pressures which he evidently so well knew how to apply.

My frigging soon brought him to a spend, and catching it all in my hands, I rubbed the creamy essence of life up and down his prick and over his balls, and even on my own cock as it drew in and out of his bottom.

My delight was perfectly indescribable. I drew it out so long, always stopping for a little when the spending crisis seemed imminent, but at last his writhings and pressures had such an irresistible effect that I could no longer restrain the flood of sperm I had tried so long to keep back, and feeling it shoot from me in a red-hot stream, the agonizing delight made both of us give vent to perfect howls of extasy.

We both nearly fainted, but my instrument was so hard and inflamed that I was a long time before it in the least began to abate its stiffness.

It was still in his bottom, revelling in the well-lubricated hole, and he would fain have worked me up to the very crisis again, but I was afraid of exhausting myself too much at one time, so gradually allowed Mr. Pego to assume his normal size, and slip out of that delicious orifice which had given me such pleasure.

A week after this first introduction Jack came again, and brought the first instalment of his rough notes, from which this MS. is compiled.

Of course at each visit we had a delicious turn at bottom-fucking, but as the recital of the same kind of thing over and over again is likely to pall upon my readers, I shall omit a repetition of our numerous orgies of lust, all very similar to the foregoing, and content myself by a simple recital of his adventures.

JACK SAUL'S RECOLLECTIONS

EARLY DEVELOPMENT
OF THE PEDERASTIC IDEAS
IN HIS YOUTHFUL MIND

Dear Sir, —

I need scarcely tell you that little cocks, and everything relating to them, had a peculiar interest to me from the very earliest time it is possible for my memory to carry me back to.

I have a brother much older than myself, and have heard him say that almost as soon as I could walk I would toddle up to anybody and ask them if they had a dilly; that lifting girls' clothes, or putting my hands on boys or even grown-up people was a regular thing with me.

My parents were well-to-do people of the farmer class in Suffolk, and I have been told of a laughable incident when I was only about six years old.

There was a family party, and at teatime my cousin

Jenny, a fine girl of about seventeen, who was slightly dis-figured by a very hirsute appearance about her upper lip, was seated opposite to me, and particularly attracted my attention, it being the first time I had ever seen her. I was so absorbed in contemplating her moustache that I could not take my eyes off her, so that she quite blushed.

At last I broke out. "What have you got girl's clothes on for? I don't believe you are a girl at all. My brother Dick has got a moustache just like yours."

"Hush, for shame, Johnny; be quiet, do," said my mother, giving me quite a severe pat, whilst the object of my remarks flushed crimson, as tears of shame started to her eyes.

"I won't. I know she's a boy. See, if I don't find out whether she's cracked like a girl, or got a spout like a tea-kettle on her!" I cried out, but was not allowed to say more, as I was cuffed and driven in disgrace from the room, whilst poor Jenny also rose from the table to retire and have a good cry over her humiliation.

About twelve years afterwards, when Jenny was a married woman, happening to be left alone with her for a short time one day, I recalled the incident to her memory, in fact I believe she never forgot it, as she used always to regard me with a most peculiar kind of look.

How she blushed at first; but putting my arms round her waist, I asked her to kiss and forgive me, if it was such a long time ago.

"You know, Jack, I will. You were such a tit then," she replied, as she permitted me to take the kiss.

"But Jenny, I love you so, and am as curious as ever. Can you forgive that?"

Her eyes looked anywhere but in my face, as she blushed and seemed deeply moved, so I redoubled my osculatory attentions till I had raised quite a storm of desire in both our heaving bosoms.

She was married to a rather old and ugly fellow, whose money had caught the silly butterfly, who thought that wealth alone could secure happiness.

You may guess the result. A friendly sofa was at hand. We sank down upon it, and, in spite of her pretended resistance, I not only investigated the crack of love but got into it. She was one of those hairy, lustful women one occasionally meets with, and when she had once tasted the fine root I introduced into her cunt (which was already swimming in spendings before Mr. Pego could present his head), she could scarcely ever be satisfied; in fact, we ran awful risks. When I was stopping in the house she would leave her husband asleep and come to my room, and when she had fairly fucked me to a standstill, would suck my prick, slap my arse, bugger me with her finger, and do everything she could think of to get even a tenth or eleventh go out of me.

I was sent to a boarding-school at Colchester when about ten years of age. Here the boys all slept by twos in a bed.

Well do I remember the first night. My bedfellow, a big boy of about fifteen, his name was Freeman, at once began to handle me all over as soon as the lights were out. His hands soon found my cock, which young as I then was, was a fine one for my age—somehow it was already stiff.

"My eyes," he whispered, "you've got a good fun. Feel mine; it is hardly bigger than yours," as he directed my young hands to another equally stiff prick.

"Rub it up and down," he whispered again; "that is what we all do. Do you like it?"

My body was in a tremble all over, and presently, as I continued the up and down motion of my hand on his cock, it was wetted all over with a warm, slimy kind of stuff which he shot into my hand.

"Don't you know what that is, Jack? Perhaps you're not old enough to come like that; we call it spendings," he whispered. "It's so nice. We often put our cocks in each other's bottoms, and spend there. Would you like to try that on me?"

At first I would not, but he at length got me to promise and try, as I should be sure to find it so nice.

He turned his bum to me, and wetting both his hole and the tip of my affair with spittle, he himself directed my cock to the place, and pushed out his arse towards me.

I did my best by shoving, and somehow it seemed to come quite natural, for I soon got in, and found my prick for the first time in a deliciously moist, warm, and tight sheath.

"Push in and out, in and out," he whispered, suiting the action of his rump to his instructions.

I liked it immensely, and clung with my arms round his buttocks, working with all my will, till at last a sudden thrill seemed to come upon me with a kind of shooting sensation in my cock. We both stopped out of breath, as if something had happened, and I suppose that was my first spend.

The other boys seemed all very quiet that first night, but the next evening, as soon as we had retired to our room, Freeman at once introduced little Jack to the other half-dozen occupants of our room (there were four beds) as a highly fit and proper chum.

"See, boys, what a fine prick the little fellow has got. He fucked my arse all right last night, and had his first spend," he said, lifting my shirt and exposing my affair, which was already as stiff as a poker at the idea of another go like the previous night.

They all crowded round to handle and admire what they called a wonder for such a little 'un.

Presently all were quite naked, each prick was stiff, and

we compared one with another. The next thing was to draw lots who should have my bottom first, and luckily for me the boy with the very smallest prick in the room drew the desired prize. He was about fourteen, but such a pretty fair little fellow that I quite loved him at once.

His first action was to come and kiss me, then with one arm around my waist, stood belly to belly, and rubbed his much smaller prick against mine.

Just then one suggested that unless we blocked up the window the light would betray us, so as they wished to retain the candles in use, they took a couple of blankets off the beds, and put them up so as effectually to darken the windows.

The next thing was to make me lean over the bed on my face, so as to offer my bottom fairly to the attack of my young lover; they next took a little pomade from a pot, and put some both on my little hole as well as the head of his prick.

Being small there was not much difficulty about his getting in, and he soon began to afford me great pleasure, especially when putting his arms round to my front, he began to frig my stiff member.

Looking round to see all that was going on, I found my lover also had one in his bottom, and the whole of them soon formed a perfect string in action, each one in the bottom in front of him, making a chain of eight links. There seemed quite a kind of electricity about it, as I fancied I felt all the pricks in my bottom by turns, and when at last it came to the spending crisis, one and all came together with cries of delight, whilst I also bedewed the hands of my partner with a few drops of spend, as I almost fainted from excessive emotion.

Of course other nights we changed places and partners, sometimes going in for a general suck all round and giving our bottoms a rest.

I got so fond of having a cock in my mouth that I could have eaten them, and at that time liked it better than anything.

I only stopped at that school a fortnight, for I was both fortunate and unfortunate at the same time.

My father was killed by accident, and mother had to take me home, because his affairs turned out so badly she could not afford to pay for my schooling; which, as it turned out, thus prevented my constitution being ruined for life by such early precocity; besides, it was all found out and the school broken up soon afterwards.

You may be sure these early impressions took a deep hold of my naturally warm disposition, although I had very few opportunities of again indulging. I knew it was wrong to do such things, and whenever I did happen to get a young friend for a bedfellow, never failed to try on for a mutual frig.

I would lay beside a fresh companion till I fairly shivered with emotion, and would wait till he was asleep, or pretended to be so, my cock all the time as stiff as a bar of iron; then my hands would slyly and gradually slip under his nightshirt, and slowly work up to the all attractive spot, gently try a few soft pressures till the cock began to respond to my caresses by a very perceptible swelling; then I got bolder, and generally my bedfellow would turn over and reciprocate my dalliances till we joined in a mutual fuck between each other's thighs, belly to belly. My favorite idea was to pull back the skin of my foreskin, and doing the same to my bedfellow's prick, bring the nose of his affair to mine, then draw the skin of mine over the heads of both cocks, and fuck each other gently so. What delicious thrills we had when spending, the seed seeming to shoot backwards and forwards from one to the other! Only those who have done it can at all realize such delicious sensations. Very seldom have I found a youth reject my caresses, although many of them would keep quite passive, and let me do everything.

Next day I could hardly ever look them in the face, but generally found them quite ready for another spree at night.

But so few chances occurred to me, and then only for a day or two at a time.

However, I met with an adventure with the other sex when I was nearly fourteen.

We had a young dairymaid about eighteen, a fine dark-eyed wench, very good looking, a strapping big, strong young woman, with rare plump arms and splendid full bosom, whilst as to her development of rump, to judge from the appearance outside her clothes, it was something superb.

My bedroom was in a garret at the top of the farm-house, and a ricketty old staircase led up to my door, and then with a twist to the other side, without any landing, you could step up to Sarah's room (she was our only servant); so it was little more than a step across from my door to hers. At the bottom of our staircase there was a door which we could bolt inside, and so be secure from burglars or the other inmates of the house, unless they fairly broke in.

Of an afternoon, after she had done milking and all her work, Sarah used to go up to her room to wash and dress, and I noticed that even by daytime she bolted the stair-case door. My curiosity was aroused, so slipping up to my room sometimes before her time for dressing, I used to take off my heavy shoes and watch her dressing through the keyhole of her door, but I never saw very much except those lovely titties and neck in the process of washing or changing her frock.

This went on for some days, and my elder brother being away at the time, I used to lay and think about Sarah for hours after going to bed; yet I dared not venture to do anything, and in fact was ignorant of almost everything about the opposite sex.

One afternoon, being rather more clumsy than usual, I stumbled against her door just as I was going to apply my eye to the keyhole, and not being fastened it flew wide open, exposing Miss Sarah in the very act of admiring her fine bosom in front of a small glass. How she blushed for a moment, but recovering herself at once, exclaimed: "Well I never, Master Jack. What do you think you will see now?"

I stammered out an excuse, but she asked me into her room, saying, with a laugh, "I know you thought you would see my legs or something, now, didn't you?"

"I know I did. You won't tell mother, will you, Sarah? I've often seen your beautiful big breasts, and wanted to see——"

"I never tell tales, Jack, if you don't. What did you want to see? Tell me," she said, with a most tantalising smile.

My assurance returned as I found she was not cross, so I told her that it was her fine bum that I so very much wished to see, adding that I would give a shilling to see it just for a moment, as I was sure it was a beauty.

"I don't want your money, dear," she replied; "but will you kiss it if I let you have a peep?"

"That I will," I eagerly replied. "Only let me lift your skirts, Sarah."

"And I must look at your's, Jack, and kiss it. Is it a bargain, dear?"

"I'll show as much as you do for a spree, so make haste," was my answer.

"What a nice little fellow you are. Give me a kiss first, and then we'll have a romp. Would you like to come and sleep in my bed at night, dear?" she asked, and I felt my breath almost sucked away, as she squeezed and hugged me to her heaving bosom. You may be sure I liked nothing better, and assured her so.

As if by magic her skirts dropped down to her heels, and in a moment Sarah was dancing round the room with nothing on but her chemise, affording me exquisite glimpses of her splendid fat bum, and a soft brown muff which ornamented the lower part of her belly in front.

"Off with your things, Jack, before I'll let you kiss me, make haste, or your bum shall smart in the twinkling of an eye," she exclaimed, dancing up to me, her rosy face all animation and a devilment in her looks I had never seen before.

My face was burning. Her daring immodesty seemed to make me quite shamefaced, and I felt so abashed I hardly knew how to speak.

"How you blush, Jack; did you never see a girl before?" she asked, seeming to take pleasure in increasing my embarrassment. She kissed me again and again, as she almost tore my clothes off, till nothing but my shirt afforded the least protection against her ardent glances.

"Slip off that ugly rag, as I do," she exclaimed, letting her chemise drop, and thus abandoning the last slight protection to her nakedness. "I must hug you to my naked body, dear; it is so nice."

"Now kiss me, and I'll kiss you," she said in a soft, excitable voice, as she pushed me on to the bed. "Your little plaything is so stiff and beautiful, I mean to fondle it, while you kiss my bum!"

I resigned myself entirely to her directions, and laying on my back on the middle of the bed, she got over me face downwards, so that her open thighs just brought a hairy covered crack right over my face and almost blindfolded me as she pressed it down to my lips, which seemed instinctively to imprint kisses on what I had just previously been almost afraid to see.

Quicker than I can put it on paper, she had hold of my standing affair. At first she kissed my belly and thighs, laid her warm cheek by the side of my cock, then I felt her kissing its head, as her hands gently drew back my foreskin, and presently I could tell that it was well in her warm mouth, and being deliciously sucked, which made me repay her in the most ardent manner possible. My own tongue visited the lips of her crack, and I sucked and thrust it in as far as it would reach.

How she sucked at my pego, as she wriggled her crack over my lips, but it did not last long before she let down a regular flood of thick creamy spendings, which so excited me that I came also at once and shot my juvenile tribute into her mouth, as she greedily swallowed every drop.

"There, there," she said, almost with a sigh, "we've done it, Jack. It's so naughty; but isn't it nice, dear?"

Then she presently slowly raised herself off my body, and we lay for a short time side by side on the bed, kissing and toying with the most attractive charms of each other's person, till at last she jumped up and begged me to dress quickly for fear mamma should be calling for us.

"Take your things, and run into your own room, and be sure not even to look at me before anyone, or it will be sure to be noticed; and you know you can come and cuddle me again all night when they are all in bed."

As I sat at tea that afternoon I could scarcely eat or drink; nothing but the delights I had tasted with Sarah and anticipations of the coming night would run through my fevered brain, whilst my poor little cock every now and then stiffened again in my breeches, till I hardly knew how to restrain my feelings.

I tried to read a fairy tale, but it was useless, and at last my mamma, noticing how I kept flushing up, sent me off to bed about eight o'clock.

Ours was an early family, everyone generally getting to

bed by ten o'clock; but how to pass those two long hours of expectation I was quite at a loss, as I lay tossing about on my bed, with one hand gently frigging my awfully stiff affair.

However, I must have fallen asleep, as I well remember waking up in the dark and feeling someone in the bed, with her arms round me, and warm lips kissing my cheeks.

"It's only Sarah, Jack. I did not expect you would go to sleep and forget me so soon. Shall I go back to my own bed, dear?" she whispered in a low voice.

"No, no. Oh, pray don't, I love you so!" I whispered in return, as I began to repay her loving kisses.

"Let us both go into my room; the bed is more comfortable for two," she said, so we at once adjourned to her apartment and were soon comfortably cuddling one another again.

"Jack," she whispered, "did you ever have any rude games with the boys at school?"

So I at once told her about my adventures, and how we used to put our cocks up each other's bottoms, etc.

I felt her actually tremble with suppressed excitement as she so nervously clasped me in her arms whilst I was telling her all about it.

"Don't you then know what a girl is like? I mean you didn't know till we kissed each other this afternoon, did you?" she asked.

"No; but I liked kissing you there, Sarah," I replied, as one of my hands indicated the spot. "May I do it again?"

"No; we'll play at mothers and fathers. You shall put your dear little prick in there. That's how babies are made by men and women, only we shan't do that," she said, as she very gently drew me upon her, and opened her legs and directed my pego to the gap of love, which was so longing to receive the little morsel.

I felt she was quite wet, and my affair glided into the well-lubricated aperture with the greatest of ease; but how deliciously warm it was! and I could feel the folds of her cunt close on my prick so delightfully that I at once began fucking as quickly as possible, glueing my lips to hers and pushing my tongue between her amorous lips, as she almost sucked my breath away. How she heaved up her bottom, and clasping her arms tightly round my slender body, kept me from being unseated by her restive steed.

"Oh! oh! oh, Jack! I'm coming, you darling—you duck of a boy, how you make me spend! Ah—r—r—r—re!" and she seemed almost to stiffen her body at the moment, whilst my cock, balls, and thighs were deluged by her thick creamy juice, which also trickled all down the crack of her bottom. Presently she recovered a little, and putting one hand down to my affair, withdrew it from her reeking cunt, and pointed it to the little hole just below, whispering as she did so, "Push in there, dear. Don't spend in my pussey, as even a boy like you might make me a baby if you come there; besides, I long to know what it is like. It must be nice, or the boys at school wouldn't do it."

"Oh! oh! it hurts though," she sighed, as I pushed on, and gradually progressed little by little; still it very evidently was anything but a painless operation, to judge from her sighs and suppressed murmurs. At last, however, I was chock-a-block, as the sailors say, and she gave me a kiss of satisfaction at having achieved our purpose.

"Now go on, Jack. It feels so nice, and excites me so."

At the same time her legs were thrown over my loins, and she heaved up her arse to every stroke of my living piston.

So tight, such a deliciously warm and throbbing sheath, delighted my little prick—I cannot describe how

I felt; but it must have swollen up immensely. It felt ready to burst, and almost directly I felt the electric shootings which give such intense pleasure in the act of emission. My very soul seemed to melt into her vitals under these blissful sensations.

"How beautifully warm; how I feel it shoot up into me! Ah, this beats everything I ever felt before!" she sighed, kissing and hugging me in rapturous ectasy.

"No, my love," I laughed. "You never felt it before when you have it in your bottom. I'm so pleased that you like our way, as I also like this little hole best."

She made me repeat the game without withdrawing, and all night long we were kissing and sucking each other's parts, till just as it was getting light we fell into a sound sleep in each other's arms.

After this first night we always slept together, but she would not always let me fuck her, as she told me too much of it might injure my health.

One morning she confided to me the secret that she often got a nice fuck in the cowhouse from our boy Joe, who assisted her in the milking. "And what do you think, Jack, I get him to do sometimes? Why, there is a long stool there which we put under one of the quietest cows that has beautiful long tits, then I lay myself on my back on the stool, and he puts one of the cow's tits right into my pussey and milks it right into me. It's beautiful, it's delicious, beats everything; no man is at all so good. It makes me come so when I feel the rush of the warm milk right up into my very womb. You shall see it, Jack, this very afternoon. I'll tell Joe you're all right, and we can have a good lark together, as your mamma is going on a visit somewhere this afternoon directly after dinner."

This was a chance for me. I had long wanted to get intimate with master Joe, who was a fine, plump, good-looking, ruddy-faced boy of seventeen, but he had always seemed so distant and shy, even to me his mistress's son; in fact it now seemed another instance of how "still waters run deep," as I thought how curious it was that he should be so free with Sarah.

As soon as my unsuspecting parent had started on her way, Sarah and I went to the cowhouse, where Joe met us with a smile of pleasure as we entered.

"Now, Joe," she said on entering, "let's get the work done as quickly as possible, and milk them all but Cowslip. Then you shall let Master Jack see how you milk her into me."

I had not long to wait, for there were only seven cows in all, and presently the long stool was placed under Cowslip, and Sarah stretched herself upon it, so as to bring her cunt just under the udder of the good-tempered creature, who seemed quite used to the trick, putting her nose to Sarah's face with quite an affectionate kind of kiss.

Joe quickly turned up her skirts till he quite exposed her belly up to the navel, then taking one of the cow's teats, he handled it a little, but not with a milking motion—it seemed to harden at once like a natural prick—and then inserting it into Sarah's cunt, he began the milking.

Her eyes seemed at once to sparkle with quite an un-usual kind of brilliancy, as she exclaimed, "Go on, go on quick; it's beautiful!" heaving up her rump as if a man was fucking her, whilst it was most exciting to see the white milk spurting from her cunt at every fresh injection, run-ning down the crack of her bottom and thighs, or hang-ing in pearly dewdrops about the silky brown moss which adorned her lovely mount.

My prick had been standing all the while I had been there, but this sight filled me with the most lustful desires, and I could also see by the protuberance of Joe's breeches that he also was in the same state, as his eyes were intently watching the operation of his hand, the twitching of her cunt, and every motion of the lascivious girl.

I fairly shook with emotion, but with trembling hands I began to undo his breeches, and pulled them down to his knees.

Heavens! what a lovely prick stood before my starting eyes!

I nervously grasped it in my hand, and kneeling down printed hot and luscious kisses on its fiery head as I pulled back the foreskin. I could eat such a delicious morsel, and longed to swallow every drop of the pearly juice I knew my caresses would soon cause to spurt from his lovely cock. I took it fairly in my mouth, sucking quite ravenously, and rolling my tongue around it in the most wanton manner, whilst my hands were busy caressing a splendid pair of balls, contained in a tightly drawn up round purse, richly ornamented with almost black hair, which hung below the root of his white and bursting shaft.

Almost with a scream, he spent at once, as he shouted in extasy, "I'm coming; oh! oh!! oh!!! you darling Jack," shoving his prick so fiercely into my mouth as almost to choke me as the hot juice spurted down my throat, to my infinite delight.

Presently he recovered a little, and changing the teats, went on milking into the delighted Sarah's cunt. She afterwards told me that the sight of Joe fucking me in my mouth seemed to double her pleasure.

Rising from my knees, I now let down my own trousers, and presented my own glowing prick to Joe's arsehole behind (for I was quite as tall as he was). He stooped a little so as to thrust out his bottom and facilitate my attack, so wetting my fingers in a pail of milk, I applied them to his fundament, moistening the head of my prick at the same time. He was evidently a maiden behind, and I had great difficulty in getting well in, but I had my arms round him, frigging his fine prick in front, and both were so excited that although I made him wince, as well as hurting myself, at last it was done.

"Ah! it's feeling nice now; push on, Master Jack. Fuck me well, frig away; I'm coming again. Oh! oh! I can't stop; do spend in me!" he cried.

Believe me, I did spend. I never had had such an emission before. It seemed to keep throbbing and shooting for ever so long, and my prick grew both in size and length that day. It had never seemed so big and inflamed in any previous encounter with boys or Sally.

Whenever my mother was away we repeated these amusements, and I often also found chances of having Joe's tight arsehole on the sly, and he also obliged me the same way, but we never told Sarah for fear she should prove jealous. In fact now and then she expressed her suspicions of my love for Joe, as naturally it made me slightly remiss in my attentions to herself.

Soon after reaching the age of sixteen my mother succeeded in getting me placed at Messrs. Cygnet and Ego's, a large West End linendrapery house, which had a most aristocratic connection.

Here morals were very strictly looked after, and it was quite impossible for the youths to indulge in any sensual amusements in the dormitories.

In a few weeks my prick became so awfully troublesome for want of employment that I often had to retire to the closet to frig myself on the sly. The sight of the many handsome girls and young fellows had a perfectly maddening effect upon me, especially as they were all forbidden fruit, and I verily believe I should have ventured to risk it with some one, if chance had not favoured me with an adventure which afforded the necessary relief.

Early one afternoon, as I was busy behind the counter, I heard some one speaking to our principal shopwalker.

"Send a good variety of patterns, Mr. Gooser, let him

bring them about four o'clock; my sister will then be at liberty to look them over."

Something seemed to strike me that I was indicated; so looking up I saw a very handsome young lady with an equally handsome man of about thirty, who was evidently her brother, speaking to the shopwalker.

"Certainly, my lord; he shall wait upon her ladyship without fail," I heard him say as he bowed them out of the shop.

Directly they were gone I received orders to go to Churton House, Piccadilly, the mansion of the Marquis of Churton, with quite a cab-load of rolls of silk for selection by the lovely lady, who I now found to be the Hon. Lady Diana Furbelow, his sister.

The portly flunkeys who ushered me up to her ladyship's boudoir were most obsequious in their attentions to me, and carried all my parcels up as well. In fact I was quite at a loss to account for such respect being shown to one who I knew in their hearts they merely regarded as a young counterjumper.

"What is your name, sir?" said her ladyship, looking up from a book which she was reading as she reclined on an ottoman in a kind of loose dressing-gown, having evidently discarded her dress after her morning drive.

"Mr. Saul, at your ladyship's service, with a lot of silks for selection from Cygnet and Ego's. Will your ladyship be pleased to have them brought up?"

"Bring them up, James, and tell William I want some wine and biscuits, as I may keep this gentleman some time making the selection. When there are so many beautiful patterns it is so difficult to make up one's mind. Pray be seated, sir, for I'm sure they keep you on your legs long enough in those nigger-driving shops."

There was an indefinable something, besides the kindness of her manners, which at once put me at my ease with this beautiful lady, and my prick was so mannerless as to stand at once under the influence of her soft, loving eyes, eyes of an etherean blue, set under a lovely pair of dark eyebrows and ornamented with a fringe of dark lashes, through which she seemed to look at you.

There was just a slight perceptible flush on her pale cheeks, and to add to the charm of her exceeding beauty, she had a splendid chevelure of really golden hair, small pearly teeth, and cherry lips, which almost made me beside myself to contemplate.

"Help yourself to a glass of wine, Mr. Saul," she said. "You must need it; besides, I am so difficult to please, you will have no easy time of it in unrolling and rolling up again all those silks you have brought. No ceremony; help yourself."

"What; not pledge me?" she said, with an arch smile. "Pour me out a glass if you please, and hand the biscuits."

The blood rushed to my face, as I stammered out my excuse that I feared to take such a liberty.

"You will very likely have to come here pretty often, so pray make yourself quite at home. Here, I wish you every success in your business. Now, sir, drink, to me!" she said, raising the glass to her lips.

I did the same, wishing her ladyship every future happiness.

She pressed me to take a second glass, and then I proceeded to open out the rolls of silk for her inspection, and at the same time I felt a most extraordinary glow pervade my whole system, as if the wine had contained some very potent stimulant.

She seemed quite absorbed in the business of selection. Her pretty hands every now and then seemed to touch me quite inadvertently; yet there was quite a magnetic influence in them—such a thrill would shoot through my frame at the slightest contact.

Very few minutes had elapsed ere she appeared to become suddenly very faint, and sank back on the ottoman.

"Oh, sprinkle my temple with water, Mr. Saul. Don't call for assistance; it will soon pass off"—as she saw me about to ring the bell. "Oh! oh! this dreadful cramp in my leg; it always comes when I feel faint. Do rub the right calf; chafe it as hard as you can," she cried out, in apparent great pain.

I sank on my knees by the side of the ottoman, and taking up her tiny right foot (I had never seen one so small before), chafed the calf as hard as I could.

I cannot describe how I felt at that moment, as my hands played over the smooth pink silk stocking which encased that delicate, but beautifully-moulded leg.

Looking up in her face, her head had sunk back on a cushion; the eyes were closed, but quite an expression of pain pervaded the lovely features.

She was insensible; what a chance! How could I resist pushing aside the slight coverings which so lightly veiled the seat of love. Heavens! she had no drawers on!

My hand stole up her lovely thigh, and was about to touch the spot itself, which I could see nestled in a little grove of auburn curls, between her closely-compressed thighs, when she seemed to awake with a sigh and a start.

"My God, what have you seen, Mr. Saul?" she said, drawing herself up and wrapping the dressing-gown closely round her.

My blood was in a boil, as I threw myself upon her, saying, in a deep husky kind of whisper, "My lovely lady, you have indeed permitted me to see too much of your charms to resist their ravishing influence. I must, I will have you, if I die for it!"

One of my legs was between hers, and I struggled to open them still more. She seemed to resist me with all her strength; we panted; we struggled; slowly but surely my superior strength seemed to prevail, the fiery head of my prick almost touched the lips of that delicious quim. I pressed my mouth to those pouting cherry lips of hers; I inhaled and sucked in luscious draughts of her fragrant breath.

Ah, ha, ha, she yields; her rigid limbs relax. I gain ground; the head of my prick enters between the throbbing lips of that heavenly cunt. I shove; I push on; it is in to the roots. Ye gods! what a paradise to enter; it seems like taking heaven by storm. The crisis seizes me, and a perfect torrent of my long-pent-up sperm floods the very bottom of her womb, and we both almost faint from excess of pleasure, and as I lay supine upon her I had the ineffable enjoyment of feeling the soft hugging pressure of those ivory arms, which now clasped me to her bosom, whilst her lips repaid my previous attentions by a profusion of loving, billing kisses.

A chuckling laugh behind me recalled me to my senses, and turning round to see what it could be, to my horror I beheld the marquis himself standing frigging a very nice fine prick of his own, and evidently enjoying the sight of our conjunction.

"There's a lewd little bitch for you!" he exclaimed. "To think of my sister, the aristocratic Lady Diana, having a linendraper's assistant; but I'll punish you. You shall commit incest with me your brother, and you, Mister Counterjumper, shall look on."

His sudden appearance had in a moment reduced my cock to its normal state of limpness, and I withdrew quite abashed from the delicious cunt I had spent in.

"Slap my arse; bugger me; shove your prick into me as I fuck her, and you shall be well paid!" he almost shouted, throwing himself on his sister, and beginning to fuck fast and furiously.

"My pet, my love, my own Diana, no one shall ever

marry you, you darling, although I must first be excited by seeing some beautiful boy have you. And you, sir, make haste to help me behind; it's the only way I can really enjoy my sister!"

Prick was ready again in less time than I can write it; the sight of a brother fucking his sister so excited me that I began to slap his bottom with my open palm as hard as I could with one hand, whilst the other was busy feeling his balls and handling the shaft of his fine stiff penis as it worked in and out of that lovely cunt.

"Fuck me! bugger me! or I can't spend!" he exclaimed, so nothing loth, I lubricated his fine hairy and wrinkled arsehole with spittle, and bringing the head of my cock to the tight-looking orifice I speedily effected an entrance.

What a fuck that was! He was evidently rather slow, although awfully excited, and both his sister and myself having just emitted a profusion of our essence of life, we were not so quick in reaching the spending point.

With both hands I frigged him, and tickled her clitoris, as he fucked away, whilst my prick was as lively as possible in his posterior aperture.

At last we came, and all three almost at the same moment; our bodies fairly quivering again and again as the electric thrills shot through our excited frames.

At last it was over, and both of them overwhelmed me with caresses till it was absolutely necessary for me to take my departure, when Lady Diana hastily selected several pieces of silk, whilst the marquis pressed a ten-pound note into my hand, and assured me I would very often have a chance of obliging both himself and sister again.

For a period of two years I continued to be their favourite, till, Lady Diana's health failing, the marquis took her to Naples.

It appeared, in explanation of this incident, that this brother and sister had always loved each other to excess since the age of puberty, and nothing would induce either of them to marry. Although the marquis at last became so blasé that he required the stimulating sight of seeing his sister fucked by a boy before he could enjoy her himself, she loved him as much as ever, and allowed herself to be used as a lure to seduce young fellows like myself, in order to pander to his depraved tastes.

I never saw the Marquis of Churton or his beautiful sister again, but a month or two afterwards I had to wait upon a rich city gentleman, the principal of a large financial house, who I shall call Mr. Ferdinand, a rather handsome but exceedingly blasé gentleman, between thirty-five and forty years of age.

Not to be too tedious with my story, I may say that I soon found out that his letch was to be frigged by a young fellow like myself, and many handsome presents did I receive from my generous patron for that and an occasional suck which I gave his prick sometimes by way of an extra treat.

Once he induced me to stop out all night, and the next day Mr. Gooser gave me my dismissal. It was done very kindly, but he assured me that the rules of Messrs. Cygnet and Ego's house could not be infringed by himself or any of the highest employés.

Mr. Ferdinand seemed rather pleased than otherwise at my misfortune, and promised to introduce me to a secret club, the members of which he assured me would only be too glad of my services at their pederastic seances, and my fortune would be at once assured.

This club was in a street out of Portland Place, and if you had looked in the London Directory you would simply have found it as the residence of a Mr. Inslip—a rather suggestive name, you will think, considering the practices of the members of his club.

I afterwards found that no gentleman was admitted

to the freedom of this establishment unless he first paid an admission fee of one hundred guineas, besides a handsome annual subscription and liberal payments for refreshments and the procuration of boys, soldiers or youths like myself.

My financial friend duly introduced me to Mr. Inslip, who was soon very favourably impressed by my feminine appearance and well-furnished implements of love.

The very same evening there was to be a club meeting, at least a dozen gentlemen being expected to be present, so after having subscribed my name to a very fearful oath of secrecy, I took my leave of the proprietor with a promise to look in and be introduced to his patrons about 10 p. m.

Just as he was seeing me to the door there was a loud knock, and he opened it to a handsome, tall young fellow, with light auburn hair and deep blue eyes.

"The very man I want," said Mr. Inslip. "Let me introduce you to a new friend. Mr. Saul, Mr. Fred Jones. Now Fred, you know we have a soirée to-night. Will you take care of Mr. Saul till then, and bring him back with you? You can let him into our ways a bit by that time, and then he will be quite *au fait*."

"All right, guv'nor," responded Fred. "I like the look of him. So come along, my dear, and have a chop and cigars at my rooms," he said, turning to me.

Mr. Jones had been a soldier in the Foot Guards, and bought out by Mr. Inslip as soon as the latter found what a useful youth he was, in great favour with the members of his club.

"We all do it," said Fred to me, as we sat smoking and sipping brandy and water after the chops he had invited me to partake of in his rooms. "It's the commonest thing possible in the Army. As soon as (or before) I had learned the goose-step, I had learned to be goosed, and enjoyed it, my dear; don't you, Jack?" he said, slapping my thigh and passing his hand over my most interesting member. "Now I'll tell you all about it. We'll keep ourselves fresh for to-night; but another day I mean to both fuck you and have you fuck me. Is that a bargain, my dear?"

Having assured him that I was perfectly agreeable to be his wife or husband, whichever he preferred, at any time, he continued:—

"I was saying how common sodomy is in the Army. Our old major was the first to introduce me to it. He made me drunk, and next morning I found myself in his bed with him. Money was everything with me then. It always has been. Why, I used to be office lad to a solicitor at Liverpool, where I forged his cheque for a hundred pounds and ran away to London, had a damned spree for a week, lost or spent it all, then enlisted. It was the safest thing to do; the military rig-out so changes the appearance of a fellow.

"Well, I was speaking about our old major. Two or three quid squared me at once, and I let him get into my arse again, as no doubt he had done whilst I was drunk. That was the first time I really felt what it was like, and enjoyed it. My stars! how the old buck afterwards sucked my prick and frigged me till I hadn't a drop of spend left in me.

"In a very short time I got used to his ways, and used to abuse him, telling him what a beast he was, etc., which used to delight him, and he would give me an extra sov. for it.

"I have had lots of women, but do not care for them, for they do not make half so much of us as gentlemen do, although of course they always pay us. You can easily imagine it is not so agreable to spend half-an-hour with a housemaid, when one has been caressed all night by a nobleman.

"This is the experience of all the men of my regiment, and I know it is the same in the First, The Blues, and every regiment of Foot Guards.

"When a young fellow joins, someone of us breaks him in and teaches him the trick; but there is very little need of that, for it seems to come naturally to almost every young man, so few have escaped the demoralization of schools or crowded homes. We then have no difficulty in passing him on to some gentleman, who always pays us liberally for getting a fresh young thing for him.

"Although of course we all do it for money, we also do it because we really like it, and if gentlemen gave us no money, I think we should do it all the same.

"Many of us were married; but that makes no difference. All we have to do is not to let the gentlemen know it, because married men are not in request.

"So far as I can see all the best gentlemen in London like running after soldiers, and I have letters from some of the very highest in the land. One gentleman, a nobleman, had me once in his own house, in the room next to his wife's boudoir. I heard her laughing, and talking, or playing on the piano, whilst her husband was on his knees before me, sucking my prick.

"We both laughed about it afterwards, especially when I asked him if he thought her ladyship would not like a dose from the same bottle?

"On one occasion five of us went with one gentleman and acted with him or with one another for him to see, every kind of buggery, frigging and gamahuching. It was a luscious scene, just such as you will see to-night, my dear," he said, squeezing my stiff prick outside my trousers. "But wait till then; don't let my talk make you randy," he continued.

"That gentleman was a clergyman, and one of the most liberal friends I ever had.

"Young fellows are quite as much after us as older men. I have often been fucked by young gentlemen of sixteen or seventeen, and at Windsor lots of the Eton boys come after us.

"I know two men in The Blues who are regularly kept by gentlemen, and one has an allowance of two hundred a year for allowing himself to be sucked.

"There are lots of houses in London for it. I will give you a list some day, where only soldiers are received, and where gentlemen can sleep with them. The best known is now closed. It was the tobacconist's shop next door to Albany Street Barracks, Regent's Park, and was kept by a Mrs. Truman. The old lady would receive orders from gentlemen, and then let us know. That is all over now, but there are still six houses in London that I know of. Inslip's Club, however, pays me best, so I am very little known elsewhere at present."

He never allowed the conversation to flag all the evening, and rattled on in the same style till nearly ten o'clock; and I think by the time we put on our hats to go to the club he had fairly told me all he knew, and considerably opened my eyes as to how the sin of Sodom was regularly practised in the Modern Babylon.

Mr. Inslip always opened the door himself, and at once ushered us into a small dressing-room, where we left our hats and other impedimenta, and under Fred's directions I assumed a charming female costume. He acted as lady's maid, fitted my bust with a pair of false bubbies, frizzed my hair with curling irons, and fixed me up by adding a profusion of false plaits behind.

Then he also dressed himself as a girl, and when we both looked in the glass preparatory to going to join the company, we appeared so pretty and feminine that I was quite in love with him, and clasped him to my breast as I imprinted hot burning kisses on his lips, whilst my hands groped under his clothes, and up his drawers, till I had hold of a splendid stiff prick. His eyes fairly shot fire as he returned my ardent kisses for a moment or two, and then suddenly wrenched himself away, with the observation that we must not make fools of ourselves. We could have plenty of that sort of thing some other time.

He had evidently heard Inslip's footstep, for that worthy appeared almost in a moment to ask how much longer we should be. He complimented us upon being two such pretty girls, and then said, "For this evening, Fred, your name is Isabel, and yours, Mr. Saul, is to be Eveline."

"Gentlemen," he said, as he ushered us into a fine large drawing-room, "these are the Misses Isabel and Eveline I had promised should be here to meet you this evening."

All rose as we entered; there were ten gentlemen and eight ladies waiting to receive us. It was a splendid apartment fitted up with mirrors all over the walls, whilst the windows were firmly closed and shuttered, besides the thick curtains which were drawn across them. Here and there were recesses filled by luxurious couches, before each of which stood a small table covered with the most exhilarating refreshments.

Two elderly gentlemen advanced and conducted us to seats.

Presently some one sat down to a piano and struck up a quadrille, and in a few moments we were going through the fascinating evolutions of a dance.

Our partners were particularly attentive to us, mine more especially so—in fact I can only speak for myself. He plied me with refreshments after every dance, and I could see was immensely taken with me. Now and then he would pinch my bottom, and after a little while slyly got one hand up my clothes and groped till he found my prick. His touch added fuel to the flames of lust by which I was already consumed; a very few touches sufficed to make me spend all over his hand, which I perceived gave him great pleasure.

About two o'clock in the morning the lights were suddenly turned out, and we were all in the dark.

"Now, love, I must have you," he whispered. "Every one has got a partner; and after I have fucked your delicious bottom, we separate and find another partner in the dark, so there can be no favouritism or neglect of any member."

He made me lean over the couch on my face, and lifting up my skirts behind he knelt down and kissed my bottom, buggering me with his tongue till the hole was well moistened; then getting up, I felt a fine prick brought up to the charge. It hurt me a little; but he was soon in, then passing his hands round my buttocks he frigged me most deliciously as he worked furiously in my bum.

How I thrust out my arse to meet every lunge! But it did not last long; we were both too hot, and came almost directly. It was a delightful bottom-fuck; but the rules precluded us from having a second, and we parted with a loving kiss, and went in search of other partners.

Before time was called about 6 a.m., I had had six different gentlemen, besides one of those dressed up as a girl. We sucked; we frigged and gamahuched, and generally finished off by the orthodox buggery in a tight arsehole.

I became a regular frequenter of Inslip's soirées, as I always got a fiver for the night, besides plenty of fun and refreshment; but contented myself with two nights a week, for fear of getting used up too soon, by which self-denial Eveline became a universal favourite.

The extent to which pederasty is carried on in London between gentlemen and young fellows is little dreamed of by the outside public. You remember the Boulton and Park case? Well; I was present at the ball given at Haxell's

Hotel in the Strand. No doubt the proprietor was quite innocent of any idea of what our fun really was; but there were two or three dressing-rooms into which the company could retire at pleasure.

Boulton was superbly got up as a beautiful lady, and I observed Lord Arthur was very spooney upon her.

During the evening I noticed them slip away together, and made up my mind to try and get a peep at their little game, so followed them as quietly as possible, and saw them pass down a corridor to another apartment, not one of the dressing-rooms which I knew had been provided for the use of the party, but one which I suppose his lordship had secured for his own personal use.

I was close enough behind them to hear the key turned in the lock. Foiled thus for a moment, I turned the handle of the next door, which admitted me to an unoccupied room, and to my great delight a beam of bright light streamed from the keyhole of a door of communication between that and the one my birds had taken refuge in.

Quietly kneeling down I put my eye to the hole, and found I had a famous view of all that was going on in the next room. It put me in mind of the scene between two youths which Fanny Hill relates to have seen through a peephole at a roadside inn. I could both see and hear everything that was passing.

Lord Arthur and Boulton, whom he addressed as Laura, were standing before a large mirror. He had his arm round her waist, and every now and then drew Laura's lips to his for a long, luscious kiss. His inamorata was not idle, for I could see her unbuttoning his trousers, and soon she let out a beautiful specimen of the *arbor vitae*, at least nine inches long and very thick. It was in glorious condition, with a great, glowing red head.

Laura at once knelt down and kissed this jewel of love, and would I believe have sucked him to a spend, but Lord

Arthur was too impatient, as he raised his companion from her stooping posture, and passing his hands under Laura's clothes, as she gave a very pretty scream and pretended to be shocked at this rudeness, he turned everything up and tossed her on the bed.

As yet there was nothing to see but a beautiful pair of legs, lovely knickerbocker drawers, prettily trimmed with the finest lace, also pink silk stockings and the most fascinating little shoes with silver buckles. His lordship quickly opened Laura's thighs, and, putting his hand into her drawers, soon brought to light as manly a weapon as any lady could desire to see, and very different from the crinkum-crankum one usually expects to find when one throws up a lady's petticoats and proceeds to take liberties with her; but his lordship's love was only a man in woman's clothes, as everyone now knows it was Boulton's practice to make himself up as a lovely girl. There seems such a peculiar fascination to gentlemen in the idea of having a beautiful creature, such as an ordinary observer would take for a beautiful lady, to dance and flirt with, knowing all the while that his inamorata is a youth in disguise.

"What's this beautiful plaything, Laura darling? Are you an hermaphrodite, my love? Oh, I must kiss it; it's such a treasure! Will it spend like a man's love?"

I heard Lord Arthur say all this, as he fondled and caressed Boulton's prick, passing his hand up and down the ivory-white shaft and kissing the dark, ruby-coloured head every time it was uncovered.

How excited I became at the sight you may be sure. I also longed to caress and enjoy both the fine pegos I had seen; but although my own prick was stiff almost to bursting, I determined not to frig myself, as I was sure of finding a nice partner when I returned to the ball-room. Still, I would rather have had Boulton than anyone. His make-up was so sweetly pretty that I longed to have him, and him have me.

But to go on, I could see that the assumed Laura was greatly agitated. Her whole frame shook, whilst one of his lordship's hands seemed to be under Laura's bottom, and no doubt was postillioning her bottom-hole; and presently, seeing how agitated he had made her, he took that splendid prick fairly into his mouth and sucked away with all the ardour of a male gamahucher; his eyes almost emitted sparks as the crisis seemed to come, and he must have swallowed every drop of the creamy emission he had worked so hard to obtain.

His other hand frigged the shaft of Boulton's prick rapidly as he sucked its delicious head.

After a minute or two he wiped his mouth, and turned Laura round so as to present her bottom over the edge of the bed, then threw up all the skirts over her back, and opening the drawers behind he kissed each cheek of the lovely white bum, and tickled the little hole with his tongue, but he was too impatient to waste much time in kissing, so at once presented his prick to Boulton's fundament, as he held the two cheeks of his pretty arse open with his hands.

Although such a fine cock, it did not seem to have a very difficult task to get in, and he was so excited that he appeared to come at once; but keeping his place, he soon commenced a proper bottom fuck, which both of them gave signs of enjoying intensely, for I could fairly hear his belly flop against Boulton's buttocks at every home push, whilst each of them called the other by the most endearing terms, such as:

"Oh, Laura, Laura, what a darling you are! Tell me, love, that you love me! tell me it's a nice fuck!"

And then the other would exclaim:

"Push; push; fuck me; ram your darling prick in as fast

as it will go! oh! oh! oh! quicker, quicker; do come now, dearest Arthur; my love, my pet! oh! oh!! oh!!!"

After seeing so much I slipped away from the keyhole, and went back to the company in the dancing room.

Park was there as a lady, dancing with a gentleman from the city, a very handsome Greek merchant, but I did not care for either of them, but sat for a while on a sofa by myself, watching the dancers and taking notice of all the little freedoms they so constantly exchanged with each other.

Presently Lord Arthur and Laura returned to the room and came and sat down by me, his lordship, to whom Mr. Inslip had previously introduced me, at once saying: "Allow me to introduce you two dears to one another. Miss Laura, Miss Eveline. I must go away for a minute, and will be back directly."

Boulton seemed to take to me at once, and after a little ordinary conversation, whispered to me as he gave me a card:

"Come and see us in our rooms to-morrow, as we are. I know I shall love you; but there is no chance for it here. We must amuse our customers to-night."

This I agreed to, and soon after the lights were turned out and a general lark in the dark took place. I do not for a moment believe there was one real female in the room, for I groped ever so many of them, and always found a nice little cock under their petticoats, most of them quite slimy with spendings, they had been frigged so often.

At last it was over, but just as Mr. Inslip was going to hand me to his brougham, Boulton asked him to let me go home with them, and at once drove me off with Park to their rooms near Eaton Square.

THE SINS

OF THE

CITIES OF THE PLAIN

OR THE

RECOLLECTIONS OF A MARY-ANN

WITH SHORT ESSAYS ON

SODOMY AND TRIBADISM

>—:0:—<

IN TWO VOLUMES

>—:0:—<

VOLUME II

LONDON

PRIVATELY PRINTED

1881

JACK SAUL'S RECOLLECTIONS
(continued)

SOME FROLICS WITH BOULTON AND PARK

As soon as we got to Boulton's place, he gave me a drop of his invigorating cordial, a lovely liqueur which seemed to warm my blood to the tips of my fingers; then we went to bed, and slept till about twelve o'clock, had breakfast, all dressed as ladies (I believe the people of the house thought that we were gay ladies).

Boulton assured me they hadn't a rag of male clothing in the place, all their manly attire being at some other place.

"I love to look like a girl, and to be thought one. I had such a lark the other day with a beautiful milliner at Richmond," he said, sipping his chocolate. "You must know I was stopping at the Star and Garter Hotel, and fancied a new dress; or, rather, I had seen this lovely milliner in her shop—she was the principal—so I went in, gave my order, requesting her to call on the Hon. Miss Murray at the hotel to try it on in two days' time.

"She was a lovely creature, nearly six feet high, but beautifully proportioned, with dark auburn hair, deep blue eyes, and such a lovely white skin, whilst her mouth was almost always on the smile, showing a lovely set of pearly teeth with which I was so much in love that I wanted to make her take my cock between her lips; besides, she was just slightly freckled, which is always a great charm in my idea.

"Miss Bruce, that was her name, called on me about twelve o'clock, as I was at breakfast, so I pressed her to take a cup of chocolate, and as I had expected her, she did not see the cordial at the bottom of the cup before I poured it out for her.

"Having elicited that she was not particularly busy, we sat chatting for some time about fashion and trimmings, etc., for I am as well up in all that as any lady in England.

"When I could see by the sparkle of her eyes that the cordial had considerably warmed her blood, I asked her to step into the bedroom to try on the dress.

"She was going to fit it on at once, and was about to remove my morning costume, when I exclaimed: 'Oh, not for a minute or two. I feel rather faint, my dear Miss Bruce. I must sit still a little. Do you mind giving me a drop of that cordial?' as I indicated a little liqueur case on the table. 'It will put me right at once. I often come over like that. Thank you. Now pray take a little yourself. It will do you good, and is so nice.'

"She followed my example, and seemed evidently to like the flavour of it.

" 'Sit down, dear, by my side. There is no hurry about that troublesome costume.'

"Then as she sat down I gave her such a luscious kiss on her mouth, saying: 'You look so pretty; do excuse me, if you won't kiss me in return. I do so love to be kissed by nice people; not gentlemen, of course, but I am so fond of ladies if they will let me love them. Do kiss me, darling!' and I drew her face again towards mine and looked into those lovely deep blue eyes.

"She threw her arms round my neck as she blushed up to her temples, and said in a soft voice: 'How can I help it? You are so loving!'

"Then our lips joined in such a long-drawn kiss that I quite felt her heave with emotion. 'Do I excite you, darling, by such kissing?' I asked, and taking advantage of her confusion, I soon had one hand under her dress, and slipped it up to the seat of love. She scarcely resisted my advances at all.

" 'You love, I must kiss it. For God's sake let me. I am so in love with you!' I said, slipping down on my knees in front of her, and before she could help herself my head was under her clothes and my tongue trying to tickle her clitoris, as my hands forced her yielding thighs apart. It was too much for her. The cordial had so warmed her blood she could hardly tell what she wanted; besides, I was a lady, and not a man, so there could be no harm in that, as she afterwards told me.

"How I did gamahuche her as she fell back on the sofa and let me have my way. She wriggled, heaved and sighed.

"I could hear her gasp out: 'You darling; you love! How nice; how delicious!'

"Then her spendings came in a thick creamy emission, and I sucked it all up, and delighted her so by the tittilations of my tongue that she soon came again.

"After a little I got up and sat by her side.

" 'And you, love, won't you allow me to kiss and return you the exquisite pleasure you have just afforded me?' she asked, as she kissed me excitedly.

"I pretended to resist her attempts to get at my cunney, and at last blushingly told her that I was one of those unfortunate beings (which perhaps she had heard of) who had a malformation, something like the male instrument— in fact, it was capable of stiffening, and always did so under excitement, exactly as a man's would do.

" 'But, darling,' I added, 'It is quite harmless, and can do no mischief like the real male affair. Now you, I know, will be too disgusted to want to kiss me, although I am dying for you to afford me that pleasure.'

"This avowal seemed to excite her still more, and she assured me that she had often heard of hermaphrodites, and that they could have women as well as a man.

" 'And now, darling, I am more anxious than ever to see and caress the jewel you must have. I own I have often wanted to feel what a man is like, and you can oblige me without any risk if you will. Will you, my darling?'

"She had got to the object of her desires by the time she ceased speaking, and at once commenced to kiss and caress it; the idea that perhaps I might be a real man never seemed to occur to her mind.

" 'Oh, do have me, Miss Murray. I should so like you to ravish me; my blood is on fire; I'm not in my right senses; the sight of such a darling fills me with such a longing that I can't restrain myself. If you don't do it for me, you shall never love my little fanny again!'

"She had it in her mouth directly and sucked it so lusciously that I felt I should spend in her mouth if I did not have her properly at once, so I jumped up and asked her to lie on her back on the sofa and open her legs well.

"She did so at once, and turning up both our dresses we were soon belly to belly; her hand kept hold of my prick and directed it to the mouth of her cunt herself.

"By heavens! she was a virgin, and so tight! but I clasped her round the waist, and pushed furiously; so much so that she fairly screamed with the pain and tried to shove me away; but the crisis came, I shot a warm flood of sperm into her tight sheath, which, besides easing it a little, so excited the dear girl that she heaved up her bottom to meet me, and as I happened to push hard at the same moment, John Thomas fairly crashed through all the defences of her unbroken hymen, leaving nothing but a bloody wreck behind, as he went in up to the hilt.

"She did not scream, but giving one long, deep-drawn sigh, fairly swooned away under me.

"I did not withdraw, but lay as lightly as possible on her, making my prick throb in the tight-fitting sheath which imprisoned it so deliciously. I could feel the folds of her cunt contract on my shaft of love with a most delightful spasmodic twitching, such as I had never enjoyed before, and in about five minutes she opened her eyes and, with a smile, whispered: 'Oh, dearest, what a dream! I dreamt I was smashed to atoms; then my soul soared away to heaven, and I have been in Paradise, tasting such exquisite sweets, such thrills of love, and now I wake up to find it is you, darling, and that dear thing of yours that gives me such pleasure. How I feel it deliciously filling every part of my womb! But you are not a man, are you, darling? you can't do me any harm, can you? Do tell me that, love, and I shall be happy; otherwise I should tear myself from your arms and burst into tears!'

"How beautiful she looked! such a lovely flush of excitement on her pretty face! how could I undeceive her, so I glued my lips to hers, as I murmured: 'No, darling; I'm not a man. I can't hurt my love!'

" 'Then, darling, give me all the pleasure you are capable of with it,' she said, smiling and heaving up her buttocks at the same time as a challenge for me to go on.

"My God! what a fuck we had! She kept me in position till I had come four times. You would think my prick would have wrinkled up from exhaustion, instead of which I was so unnaturally excited that it swelled bigger than ever, and, although I did not spend again, we kept on ding-dong till I had fairly used her up and she had to beg I would let her go, as she had no more strength.

"How many times I made her spend it would be impossible to say.

"You won't be surprised to hear that that dress did not easily fit. She came so many times to try it on, and fucked me so dry, that at last I had fairly to run away from Richmond, and she will be very lucky if she does not get a big belly."

"Have you had many adventures of that kind?" I asked.

"Yes; plenty of them. I can tell you a lot of amusing adventures; but now, Eveline, Selina and I want a bit of fun with you, all alone by ourselves. It will be real love; not the mercenary, paid love we give our customers. I have got quite fond of you, and Selina won't be jealous. She will assist to make me happy; won't you, my darling?"

He rose from the breakfast-table, and opening the piano, ran his fingers over the keys; then motioning me to come to him, gave me a luscious kiss. "You darling Eveline, I'm sure your prick stands," he said, groping under my dress and finding it was as he said.

"Now I will play you a nice piece, only I have a fancy to have you in me, and you must both fuck and frig me as I play to you," he said, as he made me sit on the music-stool, then raised my dress, and turning his bottom to me, lifted his own clothes and gradually sat down in my lap; as my stiff prick went up his bottom, my hands went round his waist, and I clasped that glorious cock of his, and he began to play and sing "Don't you remember sweet Alice, Ben Bolt?" from a parody in the *Pearl Magazine*, which he had set to music.

It had such an exciting effect on me that I shot my sperm at once, and I felt him spend all over my hands at the same time.

"Now, wasn't that nice, dear Eveline? Do you love your Laura a little bit?" he said, stopping and twisting his head round to give me a long sucking kiss on my mouth.

We kept our places, and he played several more pieces before we came again; then we adjourned to the bedroom, and he rang for the breakfast things to be cleared away.

The door was at once bolted, and then Laura asked me if I had ever been birched.

"Oh, yes," I replied; "and it's delicious when properly applied."

"Well then, Selina has not had any fun yet, and I don't think you will be any too ready to oblige her, so we intend to tie you up to the bedstead and see how soon the twigs will reinvigorate you, my darling. You know you were naughty and rude to me while I sat on your lap just now, so you must be punished for it at once."

It was useless for me to remonstrate against being tied up, as they were too strong for me, and I was soon secured by both wrists to the foot of the bed; then my skirts were pinned up and my drawers opened and let down to my knees.

"Ha, we have her now, the rude little slut!" exclaimed Laura. "Let me just pick out a proper little swishtail, and I'll take all that out of her naughty, impudent bum!"

I had never had a very severe birching, and rather dreaded they were going to be too hard on me. My poor prick had fairly shrunk up into his skin.

"Just look at that shrivelled-up thing, Selina. Did you ever see such a useless looking bit in your life? Stand clear and let me apply the reviver!"

Laura had got a long, thin bunch of birch, consisting of only three or four twigs, elegantly tied up with ribbons. Swish!—I heard it cut through the air, and if I had not been tied as I was I should fairly have jumped, such a stinging cut did I get.

"Ah! oh!! oh!!! Good God! not so hard, or you'll draw the blood!" I almost screamed out, as I winced under the pain.

"Ha! that was a beautifully practical illustration of how the birch should be applied. But perhaps you will like that better—and that—and that——?"

Three stinging cuts followed in rapid succession, and almost took my breath away.

It was no use calling out, so I fairly bit my lips to repress any cry of pain. It was not so much the weight of the blows but their smart, stinging severity. It soon made my bum all of a glow, and I began to experience a decided feeling of pleasure, my prick standing as hard as possible once more.

"Hold; hold; don't draw the blood, Laura dear!" cried Selina. "You've raised him finely. Now let me enjoy my turn; I long for him in my bottom at once. I can't wait while you play with him any longer; but you can touch him up when he is in me, to keep him to his work."

She was untying my wrists as she said this, and in less time than it takes to tell I was into her bottom and Laura's prick was in mine.

Never shall I forget the excess of lubricity of this triune fuck; we seemed all so excited; we fairly spent again and again, till nature was so exhausted that we lay in a confused heap on the bed, as our pricks soaked in each other's well-lubricated bumholes.

At last we thought we had had enough for one day and a night, so after taking a most loving farewell and promising to visit them often, I had a cab called and drove to my lodgings, where I can assure you I stopped two days to thoroughly rest and recruit my strength before venturing upon any further use of either bottom or prick.

Soon after this introduction to Boulton and Park, I had a funny adventure in the Temple. A note came from a barrister—in fact, a leading Q. C.—to say that Mr. Inslip had mentioned my name to him as likely to oblige him in a certain way, and would I be so good as to give him a call at his chambers at 4.30 p. m. next day.

Of course I went, and was shown into the private room of Mr. Horner, who I found had a lady with him.

He at once dismissed his clerk, with the observation "that he should not want him again to-day," and then, as soon as the door was closed, turning to me, said:—

"Mr. Saul, I am much obliged that you answered my

note so promptly. It is not that I require your services myself, but this lady here wants a good fucking."

"Awful! the man's mad! Pray let me out!" almost
screamed the lady in affright, as she made a rush to the
door.

"Stop her! Don't be a fool, woman!" shouted Mr.
Horner. "Didn't you come here to be fucked?—now just
answer that question—yes or no—as we say in court. Tell
Mr. Saul the truth."

The lady covered her blushing face with her handkerchief, and began to sob.

"Well I never; there's no understanding women at
all. No wonder I never got married," exclaimed the Q. C.
"Would you believe it? She came here to be fucked; I tell
you the plain truth. I wanted a nice housekeeper, a free-
and-easy one, that would humour me in anything I might
fancy, and Miss Wilson here answered my advertisement.
We were some time beating about the bush, till at last I
plainly told her she would have to stand fucking, and must
come to my chambers one afternoon on trial. She should
have fifty pounds if I did not engage her, and two hundred
a year as lady housekeeper if she pleased me. My God, I
sent for you to fuck her. I didn't mean to do it myself; the
fact is I require a very peculiar kind of excitement before
I can get a cockstand. Now, Miss Wilson, you understand
this is a nice young fellow, far nicer than myself, and I'm
damn'd if I don't see him fuck you! We'll have a glass of
fizz first, and then to business."

We had the champagne, then opening a door into another room I saw a bed. He gave me a sign, and I helped
him to strip the frightened young lady.

She was powerless in our hands, and I noticed he took
quite a particular pleasure in humiliating her and acting as
rudely as possible in every way he could think of.

When she was stripped I commenced to throw off all

my clothes, while he was amusing himself, kissing and tickling her cunt and clitoris till the poor young lady was almost dead with shame, besides being so excited that she could hardly contain herself.

"Now jump up," he exclaimed, "and don't spare the randy bitch. She's spent all over my fingers!"

Miss Wilson was too much overcome to attempt any resistance to my attack. She was not a virgin, so I soon got into possession of all she had and began to fire her blood still more by a good rapid fuck, Mr. Horner all the while slapping my arse with his heavy hand, as he laughed and almost screamed with delight.

This excited me immensely, so that you may be sure I did not spare our victim, especially as she was so beside herself with real erotic emotion that she heaved, wriggled, and squirmed about beneath me, and when the spending crisis came she was so carried away by her lubricity that her arms held me almost like a vice, and she actually made her teeth meet in the fleshy part of my shoulder.

Mr. Horner now joined in by putting one finger up my bottom, and then in a minute or two more I felt his prick take the place of his digit.

Mine was a most delightful position.

I never enjoyed anything more than I did being sandwiched between him and Miss Wilson. Not one of the three seemed anxious to bring such a delightful conjunction to a close, and I am sure Mr. H. was all half-an-hour fucking my bottom, whilst I continued to make Miss W. respond in the most amorous manner possible to the motions of my excited pego.

She so far forgot herself as to say soft endearing things, and would every now and then ejaculate:—

"Ah! oh! how delicious! You make me come again; I can't help myself. I'm in heaven. Push, push now, there's a darling!"

Whilst the barrister was so carried away that he fairly screamed with delight.

I was handsomely rewarded for my services, and he took Miss Wilson for his housekeeper, and I afterwards often went through the same performance with them at his residence in Palace Gardens, Kensington.

The next adventure I can think of was at a garden party given in honour of the Prince of Wales; I will not say exactly where, but it was in the grounds of a noble mansion on the banks of the Thames, not a hundred miles from Richmond.

Lord Arthur took me with him, dressed as a midshipman, and I was presented to his Royal Highness as the Hon. Mr. Somebody, I can't exactly remember the name now.

After promenading for some time we met an elderly gentleman to whom he introduced me as a member of Inslip's Club.

"Eveline," whispered Lord Arthur, "this is Lord H——, who has heard of your attractions; let me introduce and leave you with him."

Lord H—— expressed the great pleasure he had in making my acquaintance, adding to Lord Arthur, "that he hoped his young friend was not too shy or mock modest."

Being reassured upon this point, he took me for a walk into some of the most shady parts of the grounds.

At last we came to a very retired arbour with a seat behind some rockwork and a small fountain playing in front.

"Just the spot for us," said his lordship. "Let me sit down here and make a better acquaintance, my dear!"

He was as loving as if I had been a young girl all at once, and then as I blushed at his observations about my appearance, and the promising bunch in the fork of my trousers, he proceeded to handle me, and pressed his lips to mine in a long breath-sucking kiss.

I wished he had been a nice young fellow, but his attentions soon aroused all my usually excitable feelings—my cock throbbed, and stood as stiffly as ever under the soft pressures of his hand, as he held it inside my trousers.

"I must kiss this darling jewel!" he exclaimed. "I love to swallow all the spendings of a nice young fellow like you, Eveline."

Then going on his knees before me, he put my prick in his mouth and sucked me most lusciously, whilst with one hand passed under my bottom he postillioned me in the most delightful manner possible, and when the crisis came in a few minutes he swallowed every drop with the greatest possible relish.

His next proceeding was to lower his own breeches and get me to bugger him, which seemed to afford him equally exquisite pleasure, as his old prick stood as stiffly as possible. And after I had spent in his arsehole, he made me toss him off for a finish.

When we rejoined the company, one of the retinue of His Royal Highness begged for an introduction, and after some little conversation, assured me my fortune would be made if I would only consent to visit Berlin and Vienna, as he could introduce me to many of the highest personages in Germany.

Not caring to leave good old England, I politely declined his overtures, assuring him at the same time that I had not the least objection to be introduced to any of his eminent countrymen, should they happen to visit London.

On our return to town in the evening we found Boulton and Park waiting for us at his lordship's chambers. They wanted us to join in a special pederastic orgie, to take place the same night at the house of a certain young Earl, who had two young foreign pages just arrived, the one from France and the other from Italy, and their introduction into the mystic circle was to be the chief event of the night's programme.

Lord Arthur had another engagement, which prevented him coming with us, and so I went with them.

They had a private brougham in waiting, which took us to Grosvenor Square.

A very sedate and elderly footman ushered us upstairs to a dressing-room, which formed part of the Earl's own special apartments, a suite of six or seven rooms, rigorously set apart from the rest of the house, where none but his confidential servants and pages were ever allowed to enter.

At the time of our visit the Countess was out of town at Scarborough, assiduously carrying on an anything but innocent flirtation with a certain young Marquis; but the Earl, her husband, cared not a fig for that, so long as he enjoyed himself in his own way.

"His lordship will expect you in the billiard-room in half-an-hour. You will find your portmanteaus all right. They were placed here directly they arrived an hour or so ago," remarked the footman as he withdrew.

"Then we must not lose any time, my dear Eveline. You will find I have brought a charming costume for you," said Boulton.

Notwithstanding sundry loving jokes and liberties we were soon ready to see the Earl, and as we entered the billiard-room, found he had three other gentlemen with him, all young fellows like himself, under twenty-five or thereabouts.

"How are you, my dears? Laura and Selina, how lovable you both look; and this, I suppose, is the charming Eveline I heard so much of the other night at Inslip's. These are my regular chums, who call themselves Mr. Wirein, Mr. Cold Cream, and the Hon. Mr. Comeagain. You will, of course, find their names and pedigrees in

Debrett if you care to look them up. Now, don't be bashful, and I will also introduce you to my three pages who are in a special attendance on us to-night."

Saying which he opened the door of what looked like a large bookcase, and there stood three of the prettiest boys I had ever seen, each of them quite naked with his stiff prick in his hand.

The eldest, apparently, was a fair young French fellow about seventeen; the second an olive-tinted, but very handsome Italian boy of fourteen; and the third an exquisitely formed little nigger boy of about thirteen, with a prick that any man might have been proud of.

How I longed for the little black fellow!

The billiard-room opened into another fine apartment, used as a smoking-room, but in reality most luxuriously fitted up with most seductive-looking couches and ottomans, the heavily-curtained windows being separated by mirrors which extended from floor to ceiling.

His lordship conducted me to one of the sofas, whilst Laura and Selina took seats between the other three gentlemen.

Refreshments were served by the pages on little tables in front of us; then, at a sign from their master, they commenced a gambol at leap-frog all round the room.

This was a most exciting and beautiful sight—to see three such young Adonises flying over each other's back, all their pricks as stiff as if carved out of stone; then what a study of graceful forms the ever-varying contour of their lovely figures presented to our fascinated gaze during the evolutions of their game.

In the midst of the game Lady Isabel was announced, and I at once recognized Mr. Fred Jones, looking as beautiful as ever in his ladylike get-up.

This made four ladies and four gentlemen, besides the pages, and the Earl at once, handing me over to Mr. Wirein, sat himself down with Laura to a couple of pianos at the end of the room, and they struck up what I understood to be the "Slap-Bum Polka."

"Lay the boys across your laps, ladies, and slap them well!" exclaimed Mr. Cold Cream; so, catching hold of the little nigger beauty, I threw him across my knees, just as my partner got me on his lap, with my clothes raised and his stiff prick inserted between my thighs, one of his hands passed round under my clothes till he could get at my prick, and also frig that comfortably, whilst I turned up little Jumbo's bum and made him wriggle on my lap like a little eel at every smarting impact of my hand on his ebony posteriors.

The others were doing the same. Isabel was slapping Léon the French page, whilst Selina had Menotti the Italian, and right well did their hands bring the crimson flushes to the boys' bottoms as they slapped them as hard as they possibly could.

Our partners encouraged us by saying, "Bravo! lay on to them well: Make them spend under the slapping! Look how their pretty little pricks swell more and more at every blow!" etc., etc.

And so it was.

Then, just as we fancied our little victims really would spend their virgin essence, our partners shifted their cocks from between our thighs, and at the same time applying a little cold cream on the outside of our fundamental entrances, they slipped into our bottoms in the most delicious manner.

Mr. Wirein had a lovely prick, which just fitted me exactly, and to judge by the faces of Isabel and Selina they were equally well pleased wich their partners' affairs.

Little Jumbo's eyes were fairly streaming with tears under the pain of my slaps. I was too excited to feel the least inclined to spare that ebony bum of his, for I scarcely knew what I was doing. His cock, quite seven inches long, young as he was, so took my fancy that I quickly raised him so that he stood on my lap and brought it right opposite to my longing lips, which instantly took the coal-black head into my mouth.

Did you ever see a nigger's penis when excited? The head of it is the blackest part of his body, and looks like a bit of black marble when the skin is drawn back. I wetted one of my fingers—the middle one of the left hand—and passing that arm round his bottom, kept him steady whilst at the same time I postillioned his little bottomhole; my right hand holding the shaft of his lovely prick or playing with his balls whilst I sucked his delicious jewel of love.

My partner was equally active. His prick swelled and throbbed in my bottom as I gently rose and fell upon it, whilst the hand that was frigging me kept well to its duty.

"You darling! you love! Oh, Eveline, I'm coming! Ah—ah—there it is, my love. Can you feel it shoot into you?" he exclaimed.

My own emission came at the same moment, and thoroughly lubricated his active hand as he afforded me the most intense pleasure in both parts at once; and to add to my emotion little Jumbo shot what I believe to have been his very first spendings into my mouth. My lips closed convulsively on the head of his pego, and with a long-drawn, continued suck, drained and swallowed every drop of his virility as it gushed into my longing mouth.

When I think of that conjunction even now my prick sticks up in a moment. Never before or since has my fancy been so excited or have I so enjoyed the very acme of bliss.

The others also enjoyed themselves immensely, and the Earl had Laura on his lap as he sat on the music-stool before the piano.

Selina now took Laura's place to play to us, and all being stripped quite naked, we made five very pretty couples. The Earl had Mr. Wirein; I secured Léon, the handsome French page; Laura the little Jumbo, etc., and we again commenced a most lascivious series of evolutions, forming our hands into arches in turns, under which the others would waltz, the leading couple forming the next arch, and so on and on round the apartment, pulling, squeezing, or slapping pricks all round, so as to keep them well alive and stiff.

When tired of this we retired with our partners to the sofas, and after refreshing ourselves with wines, jellies, etc., proceeded to have each other in the most fanciful ways we could imagine.

I made Léon lay over me the reverse way, so that I could take his fine pego in my mouth and postillion him with my fingers; all of which he was nothing loth to return with the greatest of ardour, till we both came in the other's mouth and racked off each other's spunk to the last drop. Then I made him turn round facing me as I still lay on my back, and so gradually bring his bottom down on my prick till I got it all in, and had him ride me a delicious St. George, as we kissed and tipped each other the velvet with our tongues, till we both spent again—I in his arse and he on my belly, his seed shooting along all over my breast.

This rather exhausted us for a time, but we lay in each other's arms, my prick still soaking and throbbing within the tight folds of his anus, and quite oblivious to all that was passing around us, when suddenly—whish! whish! whack! whack! came a birch on poor Léon's bum, and he would have fairly unshipped my affair from its delicious berth, had I not held him like a vice in my arms.

It was his lordship, the Earl, birch in hand, whilst the Hon. Mr. Comeagain was shoving into his bottom and frigging his prick for him.

He was called Mr. Comeagain (I afterwards found out)

by his friends, as no amount of fucking ever seemed to take down the pride of his constantly standing member.

Another couple in similar conjunction were attacking with the birch the bottom of his lordship's lover, with others behind who passed their birching compliments from group to group, till young Léon's bum evidently received the quintessence of birch discipline. Heavens! how it made him move and dance on my delighted cock, whilst his affair, quite eight inches long, swelled and rubbed furiously on my belly as I lay under him.

This lasted a long time. The twigs fairly drew blood again and again, but added immensely to our enjoyment; whilst the Earl seemed to take the greatest possible delight in letting many of his strokes sting the tenderest parts of my inner thighs, and even my prick itself, if it happened to be exposed so that his rod could touch it up.

We screamed, laughed, and actually shed tears now and then, till at last it ended in the usual voluptuous emissions, which drove us almost beyond our reason from the excessive pleasure of the supreme moment.

This is only a trifle of what we went through before daylight put a stop to the further development of pederastic ideas for that time at least. All I know is that it took a good week's rest to make me feel fit to pay my next visit to Inslip's Club.

FURTHER RECOLLECTIONS AND
INCIDENTS

Only lately I have been introduced to two curious members of the Mary-Ann profession.

The first is known as Young Wilson, who is a very handsome youth of sixteen or thereabouts. He is about five feet two or three inches; very fair and pretty; with chestnut hair, dark blue eyes, and a set of pearly teeth which, combined with the rosy colour of his cheeks, makes him an almost irresistible bait to old gentlemen—or for that to young ones too—who are addicted to the pederastic vice.

We are very much in each other's confidence, so he let me into the secrets of his way of doing business.

One afternoon, as we were smoking and drinking champagne together, he suddenly commenced:—

"Do you think, Jack, I ever let those old fellows have me? No fear, I know a game worth two of that. You see, I never bring them home with me, and in fact always affect the innocent—don't know where to go to; am living with my father and mother at Greenwich or some out-of-the-way part of London, and only came to the West-End to look about and see the shops and swells, etc. If a gentleman is very pressing I never consent to anything unless he asks me to accompany him to his house or chambers. Once got home with him, I say, 'Now, sir, what present are you going to make me?'

" 'Stop a bit, my boy, till we see how you please me,' or something very like that is the answer I generally get.

" 'No; I'll have it now, or I'll raise the house, you old sod. Do you think I'm a greenhorn? I want a fiver. Don't I know too well that little boys only get five or ten shillings after it's all over? but that won't do for me, so shell out at once, or I'll raise the house, and a pretty scandal it will be!'

"That frightens them at once, so I almost always get at least five pounds, and sometimes more, as I take care to write and borrow as much as I can afterwards. There's nothing like bleeding one of these old fellows; and young ones are better still—they are so easily frightened."

He told me lots of tales of different people he had victimized in that way.

My other acquaintance, George Brown, comes on a different line of business. His plan is to pick up a swell, and ride about with him in a cab.

Many gentlemen are too nervous to take a boy home with them, or, in fact, to go to any house; but they like to get a young fellow in a cab, and either frig him or get him to do it to themselves.

G. B. would do all this, and wait till his prize was quite or nearly drunk; then rob him of his pocketbook, purse, or watch, as the case might be, very frequently even taking the rings off his fingers if he had any.

"Jack," he said to me the other day, "what a fool you are not to go in for the same lay as I do. You would get hundreds where you now only get tens.

"I had a rare lark with a Jew the other day. I knew he belonged to some City financial firm. He was too fly to get drunk; but took me down to the Star and Garter at Richmond on a Saturday afternoon (no doubt he had been to his synagogue in the morning). Well, we had a first-rate dinner, and by way of dessert I handled and sucked his rather worn-out prick till he spent, and he did the same to me; but I don't like Jews—they are so dark-complexioned, and both taste and smell rather strong—so I made up my mind to make him pay well for it.

"At length when he ordered a last bottle of fizz, and

took out his purse to pay the bill, I could see he had very little more than a tenner left, which no doubt was intended for me; and so it was. Directly the waiter was gone out of the room, he tossed it across the table to me, saying: 'There's a little bit of paper for you, George. It's good pay for an hour or two, my boy. I wish I could make money as easily!'

"Of course I pocketed the flimsy; but never made any remark, except: 'Is that all for what I have let you do?'

" 'Why, you don't even thank me for being liberal!' he remarked rather angrily.

" 'Nothing to thank you for; I could wipe my arse on that! I mean to have a cool hundred; as I know it's nothing to you, who can swindle more than that any day in the City. Shall I call at your Cornhill office for it on Monday, or will you give me an I. O. U.?'

" 'You bugger! You shan't have a damn'd penny more!' he growled out, putting on his hat. 'I'm going!'

" 'Not till you square me, Mr. Simeon Moses!' I said, speaking as loudly as possible. 'You know you have been acting indecently towards me, and showing me a volume of the "Romance of Lust!" Would you like a bobby to find that book on you?'

"You should have seen him start as I mentioned his real name.

" 'Hush! hush! for God's sake speak a little lower! What do you want? I'll send you the money.'

" 'No you won't! I'll call for it anywhere you like to leave a hundred quid for me; but you must give me the rings off your fingers as security, to be returned when I get the money, on my word of honour.'

"He was too frightened not to comply at once, and told me to take them to a certain house in a little street out of Harley Street, any time after ten o'clock the next Sunday evening.

"I knew the house very well. It was kept by a great big bully, who had been a soldier, so, thinking perhaps there would be a little trouble in making him hand over the tin, I borrowed a small life-preserver from a friend by way of precaution, then went for a settlement.

"The bully opened the door himself.

" 'Has Mr. Simeon Moses left a hundred pounds for me?' I asked.

" 'Your name's George Brown, I think. Step into the parlour, and I'll see you presently,' he growled.

"Half-an-hour passed, and he still kept me waiting, so I gave a furious ring at the bell, which brought him in swearing at me for my damn'd impudence.

" 'Now, Bill Johnson—you see, I know your name, and what's more, I know the games you carry on here—no humbug!' (bringing out the life-preserver and striking the table so as to make a regular mark in the mahogany). 'Have you got the money or not? I shan't stop, and Mr. Moses may whistle for his rings if I don't get it now!' I said, speaking loudly.

" 'Damn it! yes. Only don't make a row. But he told me only to give you ten pounds and keep the rest!'

" 'Give me ninety and keep the ten. I don't mind a fair commission,' I replied, and so we settled it at once, and had a good laugh over the sodding fools, as I stood a bottle of fizz."

After telling me the foregoing tale, he went on:—

"Did you ever hear that I was four years in the Reformatory at Red Hill? That was where I first had a prick up my arse."

"No," I replied. "But do you mean to say such things can be done there?"

"Yes," said George; "and if it had not been such a hell of a place I should have been a good scholar. Of course, the boys are supposed to go to school and work in the grounds. As for work, it was nearly all play; and none of us cared for the good-natured old schoolmaster, and so never learnt much.

"As to the sleeping arrangements, I was in what they called a dormitory—it ought to have been called a back-door-mitory. There were over twenty of us boys and lads in the one large room.

"As soon as we were locked in for the night, one of the biggest of them, observing me for the first time, says: 'Hullo! here's a greenhorn. We'll soon make a free-man of him!'

"They crowded round me, just as I had almost got my clothes off ready to get into bed with another of about my own size (I was fifteen).

" 'What's your name?' 'How long are you sent for?' 'Have you ever had a cock up your arse?' etc., etc., was asked by one and the other of them, and they soon found out that in the latter respect I was quite innocent.

"In a trice I was thrown upon the bed, and held down on my back whilst all of them spat on my prick to make me a free-man; so, knowing it was useless to resist, I took it all as good tempered as possible, and hoped it would soon be over. But I was soon undeceived, for they proceeded to spreadeagle me on the bed, face downwards, by tying my wrists and ankles to the four corners of the bedstead; then a couple of pillows were pushed under my belly, so as to raise my bottom up a little. Then the biggest boy got up behind me and put his stiff prick to my arse-hole.

" 'Ah! oh! oh!! you hurt. I won't stand that. I'll tell the master in the morning!' I screamed out, and then began to cry.

"In an instant they tied a handkerchief over my mouth, whilst someone got hold of my prick, all greasy and slimy as it was from the spitting, and began to frig me, whilst the one behind me was trying to get his tool in.

"He pushed and pushed. It was impossible for me to scream, yet it was like forcing a bar of iron up my bottom. The pricking and stretching sensation was awful, and I do believe I should have been greatly injured if he hadn't spent his juice, and so eased the passage a bit. This enabled him to get right in, and I could feel his prick swelling and palpitating inside my bottom, whilst I felt so stretched and tight that I was really afraid for him to move.

"However, the feeling of distension went off after a bit, and it began to feel far nicer, especially after a few gentle moves on his part; then presently he spent again, and it felt so lovely and warm and nice, as it shot up into me; so much so that I began to wriggle about under the curious and pleasurable sensations he had aroused within me. My blood was on fire, and tingled in my veins to the tips of my toes and my finger ends, whilst their delicious frigging made me spend all over the pillow under my belly.

"The captain of the room having thus opened up my virginity, as they called it, had to withdraw; then one after the other got into me, and spent so quickly that it oozed from my bum and ran down the cheeks of my bottom, over my balls, etc. I was perfectly inundated with the slimy mess, but enjoyed it immensely; such a succession of stiff pricks revelling in my arse excited me so that I came again and again, as they continued to frig me; till at last the gag was removed from my mouth, and I was asked if I would tell the governor now, and as soon as I answered, 'No,' they let me loose.

"All night long the boys kept the game up, either fucking each other or sucking one another's pricks, and I can assure you I thought it was a beautiful game, which quite reconciled me to the confinement.

"Sometimes a new boy would be obstinate; then he was sure to be treated with the greatest possible cruelty.

They would tie him down as they did me, and then flog his buttocks with a pair of braces with the buckles on till his rump was as raw as a beefsteak.

"It would take days to tell you of all the sprees we had at Red Hill.

"There was one young fellow, who, being rather of a superior education to the rest, was made a junior teacher in the school. Well, do you know the boys of his class would actually frig him as he sat at his desk to hear their lessons, for the head schoolmaster was mostly asleep, and no one else dared say a word. This fairly broke his health down, and he had to go into the infirmary.

"What games there used to be in the kitchen! The head cook was a great, strong woman of about forty, and had another woman almost like herself as assistant, and they were allowed half-a-dozen boys to help them. They were not always the same boys, but every morning the head cook would select those she liked, and march them off to the kitchen, so as, she said, to give every one a turn—and a good turn it was. We had to fuck both the women. They would each of them do the whole half-dozen, and fairly fuck us dry, and I have seen the boys throw them down and slap their fat arses till they screamed for mercy; then we would bugger them and frig them till they almost fainted from exhaustion.

"I don't mean to say that this was done every day, but perhaps once or twice a week, when they knew the governor was gone out. He used to come round first, and then as soon as he was gone the spree was started."

A few days ago George Brown, when a little under the influence of Bacchus, let me partially into another secret of his, which affords a partial clue to how so many unaccountable mysterious disappearances are always being mentioned in the papers.

"Do you know, Jack," he said, "what I do when things

are a bit slack? I can always earn a poney (twenty-five pounds) if I take a little girl of about fifteen to a certain house in Paris; in fact, they will give me an extra fiver for every year she is under that age, so that a girl between eleven and twelve is worth forty pounds and all expenses paid. Now and then I get them a boy for a change, as they are in great demand for the rich visitors to Paris, especially for the Americans, who are nearly all sodomites. You heard of the case of General Ney, who shot himself the other day? Well, he was a regular customer to a certain Mme. R—— that I know, but they were too greedy, she and her ponce; always wanting money, and threatening the General to tell his wife and mother-in-law if he didn't shell out, so at last the poor fellow blew his brains out. If the boys or girls turn out obstinate, they are outraged with brutal violence, and then disappear no one knows how, but I have nothing to do with that.

"A fortnight ago I went down Whitechapel way, and dropped on to such a nice, pretty boy. He was a shoeblack, and, although only about thirteen years of age, beautifully formed and well hung with fine light golden hair, blue eyes and cherry lips. I fell in love with him myself. Whilst he was blacking my boots I asked a lot of questions about what he earned, etc., and soon found that he lived in a refuge, where they kept nearly all he brought in every night to pay for his schooling and board, etc., as he had no parents or relatives of any kind.

"Here was a chance for G. B., so I soon got him to promise to meet me near Moses' shop in Aldgate in the evening, and the result was I bought him a rig-out as a page, had his ragged school livery made up into a parcel and sent back to the refuge, and took him off in triumph to my lodgings, a fresh place I engaged for that purpose that very afternoon. He was my page, and had a little bed made up in an ante-room next my own bedroom.

"I had four rooms en suite at three guineas a week in a nice street in Camden Town.

"Next day I bought him some more clothes, shirts, hose, etc., and had him well bathed; in fact, he made a handsome little gentleman when dressed in mufti.

"He seemed delighted at the change in his prospects, and the jolly blow-out of good things at every meal; so in the evening, after supper, I asked him how he would like to go back to the Ragged School Refuge again, as I did not think I should keep him very long.

"You should have seen the tears come into his beautiful eyes, as he threw himself on his knees and begged I would keep him, that he would die for me, and do anything he could to please me.

"It was some time before I would appear at all moved by his appeal; then I said: 'Well, Joe, will you promise never, never, to let out any of my secrets or what games I may play with you? Now swear it, sir, on the Bible!'

"So I made him take a fearful oath, which I felt sure had a great effect on him after his Sunday School teaching.

" 'Bring me that small bottle of liqueur off the sideboard, Joe,' I said, as soon as he had taken the oath. I had a little of it in some water myself, and gave him some. You know, Jack, the stuff it is, and what an exciting effect it has upon everyone.

" 'Now I want to examine your figure,' I said, 'because I won't keep a boy unless he is well formed everywhere; so just strip yourself, my lad.'

"I should not have thought he had so much sense of decency; but he blushed as scarlet as the most delicately bred youth could have done, and the sight perfectly delighted me, as it was a proof of his being a real virgin as yet.

"However, he did not hesitate, although the wavy blushes kept flushing across his pretty face as he threw aside his clothes, and presently stood quite naked before me, whilst the liqueur had such an effect that his fine little cock, quite six inches long, was as stiff as a ramrod, and evidently caused him considerable embarrassment.

" 'Come to me, Joe. You look all right; but I must feel you all over, to see if you have any blemishes. How's this?' I exclaimed, touching his prick with my hand. 'Is it always sticking up like that? Put your hand into my trousers. You won't find me so. It's awfully rude, sir!'

"He was afraid of displeasing me, or I should never have got him to unbutton my trousers and put his hand on my prick; but he did, and pulled it out to view, as I ordered him to do. It was limp, but I knew his touch would have the magic effect very soon.

" 'There, sir,' I said, 'why are you different to me? See if you can make me the same. Take the head in your mouth, and draw back the skin.'

"I could see he did not like it, but did it to please me. The touch of his warm lips and the soft pressure of his hand brought me up in a moment. It quite filled his small mouth; but I placed my hands on his head, and ordering him to suck it, and tickle it with his tongue, kept him to his task till the crisis came, and I almost choked the pretty fellow with my spendings.

" 'Ah, oh, delightful! It's heavenly, Joe. If you please me like that I'll never part with you, my dear boy!' I exclaimed, carried away by my feelings. 'Here; kiss me, my dear boy!' as I raised him on my lap, and glued my lips to his, sucking my own spendings out of his mouth. 'It was so awfully delicious, Jack!'

" 'Did that give you such pleasure, sir?' he asked in a kind of whisper.

" 'Yes, Joe, my darling. I'll make you feel the same for yourself presently,' was my reply. 'You shall sleep with me, and we will now go to bed as soon as I am undressed.

Take your clothes into your own room, and come back to me naked, just as you are.'

"We both got on to my bed in a state of beauty unadorned, and I sucked his little cock till I felt sure he must come soon, then, kneeling up on all fours, I ordered him to shove it into my bottom. He was too excited not to be ready to do anything I told him at once, and besides, there was no difficulty about his getting into me, as I could take a much bigger affair than his. Still, my fancy was awfully excited at the idea of having his virginity, and to think that his maiden spend would be in my arse.

"The little fellow came quite naturally to the business, and fucked me so beautifully that I spent in his hands as they clasped round my body and held my prick as I had directed him to do; then presently his shoves became more rapid and eager, and I felt his warm sperm shoot right up into me in a delicious jet of love juice, as he almost fainted on my back from the excess of emotion it caused him.

" 'Oh! oh! what is it? How funny, how nice to feel so!' he ejaculated, between laughing and sighing. 'Oh! I suppose that it's the same kind of pleasure that you felt when I sucked you.'

" 'Now, Joe,' I replied, 'you know what it is like, you will let me do it to you. Isn't it beautiful?'

"He kissed me, and told me I might do anything I liked with him, he loved me so; only he feared my big affair could never be got into his small bottom, and I could see he was rather afraid of the attempt. But I soon reassured him, and got him to kneel up for me as I had done for him, then, anointing the delicious looking pink hole with some cold cream, I brought Mr. Pego to the charge. At first I could make no impression; but having got my finger in, and opened up the way a little, I succeeded in getting a slight lodgment, which made him scream with pain and apprehension, especially when I began to push on a little further.

" 'Ah! oh! dear sir! Oh! oh! pray don't; you'll split me! Oh! oh!' etc.

"Being afraid his cries would be heard, I reached a pocket handkerchief, and before he knew what I was about, had him effectually gagged.

"It was managed without losing my place, then with one hand putting a little more of the cold cream on the shaft of my prick, I gave a tremendous shove, and got a little further in. It must have been awfully painful, for he writhed and struggled to free himself from me, and went flat on the bed with a deep sigh, which would have been a scream but for the gag.

"The fact that I was inflicting awful pain only added to my lust, and regardless of consequences I pushed on till his virgin bottom had been completely ravished, and I could see little drops of blood ooze from him at every motion of my prick, which was also stained with blood, sperm, etc.

"I had spent; but the idea was so exciting that I kept on till I had done it three times, and the tight aperture became quite easy, and I felt the gag might be removed with safety.

"From what I could see of his face he was both crying and laughing in an hysterical state, so I thought I had better stop for that night at least, and it was a long time before I could bring him round to perfect sensibility.

"I had him again the next night, but it was awfully painful to poor Joe; then I took him to Paris and sold him for a hundred pounds—he was so handsome I wouldn't take less.

"Did you ever hear there is a small and very select club in Paris, where they practise every kind of cruelty, and even sometimes kill their victims. That's where, I believe, the refractory victims are finished off, but I don't know much for certain."

There are many more like young Wilson and George

Brown, who have particular specialities for turning the pederastic vice to account, but I will now go on with my own experiences:—

Not long ago I had a rather mysterious note, asking me to call upon a gentleman at his chambers in Brook Street, Grosvenor Square. I soon found out that he was a young nobleman of great wealth, so made up my mind to wait upon him. He went by the name of Mr. Carton, and received me so graciously, and without the least ostentation, so that I was perfectly at ease with him from the very first moment.

"I heard of you, Mr. Saul, from a friend of mine who is a member of a certain club you visit. They call you Eveline, do they not?" he remarked, as soon as I had taken a seat.

Receiving my affirmative reply, he went on: "Then we perfectly understand each other. I require your assistance in a little delicate business, which I would not mention had I not been very well assured of your discretion. Of course, you know, I shall pay handsomely. The fact is I come of a very curious family. Both my father and mother (whom I need not mention) had most peculiarly erotic fancies, so I suppose that it is born in us. I am the youngest—not yet attained my majority—and have two sisters, one twenty-two and the other twenty-three years of age, and as beautiful as they are amiable, yet as lustful devils as angels can by any possibility be. The eldest seduced me, her brother, before I was sixteen, and soon let her sister into the secret.

"They are too wise to be fucked in the regular way. (God only knows how they came to know so much, but I suspect our French master, as he taught me a thing or two besides my lessons.)

"Well, as soon as they had made me their own, I had to bugger them, or let them gamahuche me, whilst I did the same to them. It has gone on for a long time. They are both considerable heiresses, and determined never to marry and lose their liberty, but they find me quite insufficient to keep pace with their lustful ideas, so I want you to give me your assistance.

"We have got the most beautiful dildoes possible to be obtained in Paris, with which they fuck my bottom, whilst I do the same to either Emma or Eliza, as the case may be; but we are all of opinion that the real living instrument is so much to be preferred. By the bye, did you ever fit on a dildoe just above your own prick, and fuck a girl with it in her cunt, whilst at the same time you bugger her bumhole with your pego? That is what I often do for them, and I think it must be awfully delicious, to judge from the state of excitement it throws them into; and besides, I myself, by stretching the imagination a little, fancy it is a real man's prick which I can feel rubbing against mine, with only the thin membrane (almost as fine as a French letter, which you know is the sole division between the two holes), between the two pricks. It's so delicious!

"You make up as a beautiful girl, and let them find out your male furniture as the game developes itself, and let the direction of affairs take its chance. They have a fancy for indulging in a little flagellation this evening if I can procure them a subject. They have read so much about it in books, especially in the "Birchen Bouquet," that they think it will add materially to their lustful appetites if they can flay a girl's bum by way of a prelude. You will catch it smartly, but the guerdon shall be equal to the pain. Are you agreeable? If so, go home and dress; then be here about 10 p. m. You will be shown up at once. Take the name of Miss Eveline Birch if you like."

He gave me a fifty-pound note, and said he hoped I would be punctual to the time named, which I assured him I would be.

I had enjoyed the thrilling effects of the rod too well when administered by Boulton at his apartments, so I now readily agreed to Mr. Carton's proposal, who, when I returned at the appointed time, I found with two beautiful young ladies.

"Allow me to introduce you, Miss Birch," he said, placing a chair for me, "to my two sisters, Lady Emma and Lady Eliza Carton. My dears, this is Miss Eveline Birch, the naughty girl who has come to be punished. Her papa and mamma have given me carte blanche to whip her till she confesses her liaison with a young officer in the Guards and promises never to speak to him again. Won't it be fun, dears? But not for her. I rather guess it will be a serious business for her delicate etceteras; you understand what I mean."

"Then don't give her time to think about it," said Lady Emma, as she and her sister rose in a very stately manner from their seats. "We are going into the next room, and shall be ready for her in two or three minutes. You had better give her a glass of wine to keep up her spirits."

I had hardly time to swallow a second glass, as Mr. Carton said they meant real business and would be back in a jiffey, before they threw open the door and reappeared, each of them having discarded her dress. They had only on their white petticoats, set off by handsome corsets, which displayed all the glories of their splendid bosoms to the best effect; and when I add that they were both lovely brunettes, with blue-black hair, dark hazel eyes set under splendidly arched dark eyebrows; long, drooping eyelashes; cheeks like a mixture of milk and roses; and the whole set off by ruby lips and pearly teeth, you may imagine it was a sight to move St. Anthony himself, especially if he could have caught a glimpse as I did of fine knickerbocker drawers, trimmed with costly lace, and lovely legs and feet in white silk stockings and Parisian boots, high-heeled and sparkling with diamond buckles.

Each had a lovely swishtail of birch in her right hand; not heavy rods, but just four or five pliant twigs of considerable length, elegantly tied together with blue velvet and magenta ribbons.

Advancing to me, "Come, Miss Eveline," said Lady Emma, "allow us to conduct you to punishment. We have a nice ladder in the next room, and our brother here shall enjoy the sight of your humiliation and disgrace."

"You shan't whip me! I didn't know what I was sent here for. No; indeed I won't, ladies! touch me if you dare!" I exclaimed. "Let me go! I've had enough of such nonsense!"

"Here, Walter, help us," they appealed to their brother. "She shall soon change her tune, the impudent hussy! What a joke to think she didn't expect it!"

Mr. Carton, who had placed himself before the door to prevent my attempted retreat, threw off his coat, and then all three seized and dragged me, in spite of my pretended resistance, as I cried and screamed by turns. Their excitement seemed to give them extraordinary strength, and I was soon fastened up by my hands to the ladder, and my dress, all in tatters from the struggle, was at once pinned up round my waist, then my drawers were opened behind, just as I found one ankle tied by some kind of cord to the bottom of the ladder.

"That's right, Eliza," cried Lady Emma. "Leave the other foot loose. Now the wicked girl shall get her desserts—my arm shall ache before I give over whipping her! What a horribly fast girl she must be to flirt and go on with officers of the Guards! How do you like that, Miss Eveline? and that? and that?" giving my poor bum three terribly sharp cuts.

I bit my lips to restrain any cries.

"Ha, you don't speak. Just let the naughty girl's drawers down to her knees, will you, Eliza dear?"

"Why, she's a man!" almost screamed Lady Eliza, when the drawers were let loose. "Look, sister! look! Don't spare the horrid creature!"

They both blushed deeply, especially when they saw that their brother had prepared a surprise, and was rather enjoying their confusion.

Lady Emma muttered something about "Dirty wretch, I'll pay him out!" and then, suddenly recovering herself, rained a perfect shower of cuts on my poor rump, whilst Lady Eliza, also seemingly in a great rage, took up another rod and helped her sister to cut me up.

How I screamed, and fairly yelled for mercy. "Oh, for heaven's sake, do, do forgive me, ladies! Your brother made me do it, and now sits there laughing at me! I beg your pardon. Oh! oh! oh! indeed I do!"

Mr. Carton was almost beside himself with excitement, and had got out his prick to frig himself. It was a beautiful specimen, about eight inches long, with a fine ruby head.

Their blows never relaxed; the small tips of the twigs cut round my buttocks till I was fairly excoriated and bleeding all over from the small of my back to the middle of my thighs, and the blood trickled down my legs, whilst neither prick nor balls escaped their merciless attack. Still, it was not so awful as one would imagine. The pain soon became dulled, and then was succeeded by a beautiful glow; such a lovely sensation—it is almost impossible to describe—pervaded my whole frame, and they must have seen it indicated in my face, for, throwing aside their rods, they let me loose, and embraced me with tears in their eyes.

Mr. Carton threw off all his clothes, and tore off the petticoats and every rag of covering from his two beautiful sisters.

Lady Emma was my mark at once, for she threw herself over a bed, projecting out her rump, which I considered an invitation to me to attack her lovely bottom. My cock was in such a furious state of lust and so distended, but I never gave that a thought.

How she winced as she first felt the hot head charging the tight little brown hole! but putting one hand behind her with a little cold cream on one finger, she greased the end of Mr. Pego; then, taking him in hand herself, directed my engine of love to the wrinkled entrance.

How bravely she met my attack; but it was soon effectual, and I glided into Paradise—such a warm, tight, juicy sheath throbbed upon and held my delighted prick! I was going to enjoy the sense of possession for a few moments, but was startled by a smart attack on my own sore bum; the cheeks were pulled apart, and I felt the head of Mr. Carton's affair battering for admission; then one hand was passed round to my front, where it groped to feel how I was getting on in his lovely sister.

This made me look round, and I then saw that Lady Eliza had fitted on a dildoe, and was just ready to get into her brother's bottom. What a luscious scene that was; and how lovely the two aristocratic young ladies looked!

He was into me in less time than I can write it, and the exciting effects of the previous flagellation made me almost beside myself. Each shove I gave into the bottom of the lovely Lady Emma I had a corresponding one from her handsome brother, who was pushed on to do his best by Lady Eliza behind.

A very few of these thrilling motions brought us all to a crisis. I felt his warm sperm shooting up to my very soul, just as my own spendings did the same for his sister, and we kept the same position till we all came together again.

After this luscious bout the two sisters sucked our pricks till we were as stiff as ever, then each of us fitted on a dildoe, and had them so in both holes at once, but I had the Lady Eliza for a change. Giving full scope to my imagination in this conjunction, I fully realized all the delights of which Mr. Carton had spoken at my first interview with him. It was indeed delicious to feel, as it were, two pricks rubbing against each other inside the dear girl, with only the thin membrane between them.

After this we made the two sisters lean forward and present their posteriors over the edge of the bed; then we made both of them feel a little of the realities of birching, till they fairly cried for mercy, and begged us once more to let them have our dear pricks in their bottoms.

That is how we passed the first night, and ever since I have been quite a favourite with them and their brother.

THE SAME OLD STORY

ARSES PREFERRED TO CUNTS

Since Nero had his mother, and Caligula fucked his horse, I believe that incest, sodomy, and bestiality have been fashionable vices.

I know one man, a Q. C., who regularly keeps a goat, which he prefers to either man or woman.

Another, a young nobleman of twenty, acts the part of Oedipus, and is passionately in love with, and fucks his own mother. Still, no doubt sodomy bears away the palm over all other vices.

I know a recent case in which a widow, keeping a small shop near Leicester Square, had a lodger who occupied her first floor for the last three years. Recently one evening after shutting up, she fancied she heard a noise in the front passage, but could see nothing, so as the man who usually put up the shutters for her had not gone, she asked him to wait a little while in the kitchen and listen. After about half-an-hour he fancied that he heard shuffling and whispering in the passage, so taking off his boots, he crept softly upstairs, and suddenly striking a match, saw Mr. Parsons, the first floor lodger, in the very act of getting into the bottom of a soldier, who had his breeches down and at once bolted out of the door without waiting to put himself in decent order. The lodger slunk upstairs, and took his leave next day.

Just as this is going to press there is a case in the London *Daily Telegraph* of July 9, 1881, in which a corporal of the Scots Guards is caught in the act of committing an unnatural offence at a coffee house in Lower Sloane Street. He gets committed for trial, whilst his companion, who has the luck to be Secretary to the German Embassy in London, is claimed to be dealt with by the German Government, and sent home to Vaterland, which is no doubt all that will happen to him.

The prevalence of sodomy amongst schoolboys is little suspected of being so general as it really is. Only lately a medical man of large practice was called in to consult with the master of a large academy, where it appears the scholars had learnt something much more interesting than Latin or Greek. His tale is given just as he related it to the doctor.

"A day or two ago, sir, my suspicions were aroused as to something highly improper going on in the sleeping rooms at night, so I determined to find out all the facts by ocular demonstration. Having several vacancies in the school, there happened to be a small room of three beds quite empty.

"This I availed myself of, and on Wednesday afternoon, when all were out in the cricket-field, I made some peepholes, so that they gave me a full view into two rooms on either side.

"The little room was supposed to be locked up, and also the master (myself) was thought not to be at home; so I slipped upstairs a couple of hours before bedtime, and locked myself in.

"By-and-bye they all came laughing upstairs, accompanied by two young ushers, one of whom slept in each room to keep order.

"By standing on the beds I had a full view of everything going on.

" 'Now, Mr. Smith, let's see if your prick is sore after having three of us last night!' I heard one of the biggest boys say, and looking into the room, there was a rare romp going on. Four boys had thrown Smith on a bed, and were trying to unbutton his trousers, and at last got out his cock—it was a good size, and stiff as possible. I then saw Charley Johnson, a boy of fifteen, take it in his mouth and suck it, whilst another boy did the same with his pego, and so on till every one but the usher had a prick in his mouth.

"I was too spellbound by the sight to make a noise or interfere. The fact is, doctor, I couldn't help frigging myself; and we all seemed to come at the same time.

"After this they began to quietly undress, so I took a peep into the other room, and there, by God, sir, the boys were fucking each other's arses! It drove me nearly wild. If I don't stop it they will draw me into their practices, and I can't resist the temptation my peepholes afford; so what is to be done I don't know. Besides, my school would be ruined if it were found out."

The doctor advised the schoolmaster to have every one, ushers as well as pupils, medically examined one by one, and then he (the doctor), would pretend to find out from appearances all they had been doing, and try to frighten them out of doing it again by describing all the awful effects of pederasty.

Wouldn't many of our readers have liked the doctor's job?

A SHORT ESSAY ON SODOMY, ETC.

Sodomy appears to have been one of the most important of the Roman vices and amusements; it was not by any means considered improper. We are speaking of sodomy with males, for we do not find anything much said about sodomy with women in the literature of the Roman day.

We say now a woman is all cunt, and the Marquis de Sade says that he must be a beginner indeed who has not had a boy, or made a boy his mistress. Martial treats sodomy with women good naturedly, and no doubt the Romans practised it. Many moderns are given to having women in the bottom, and most men who have gone in for anything like dissipation have done it now and then, and we sometimes hear of marriages being made unhappy from that unfortunate taste in the husband; but we think that with modern Europeans (except in Turkey, Greece, and part of Italy) it is quite the exception to find a man wedded to that practice; but with the ancient Romans it must have been a vice too common to be even alluded to.

If women are all cunt now what must they have been then?

Sodomy with males, with the above exceptions, is still rarer in the present day, and although we have made the most careful research, we do not know of many professional male sodomites in London; and when we were boys we remember a gentleman who kept a tall young fellow, a Creole, near Leicester Square. Our criminal reports show that such things do take place, and it is not long since that I was in court and heard a gipsy found guilty, first of all of having his own donkey, and afterwards a neighbour's little boy.

The offence is common in France. Ambrose Tardieu speaks of having investigated two hundred and seventeen cases of passive sodomy—not always cases of French subjects—and speaks of the extraordinary enlargement of the *sphincter ani* arising therefrom. The vice is evidently attractive, from the number of things different admirers of it have inserted in their anus, in default of something better, such as knitting-needles, bottles and glasses; and he especially speaks of bottles of Hungary waters and eau de Cologne being inserted in the bottom-hole, also pieces of wood, and he mentions that in the latter case the whole fist of the surgeon could be introduced into the anus.

Another person, for a bet, put a tumbler up his bottom; and two children, the brother five years old and the sister seven, were caught one day putting spoons, carrots, and potatoes up each other's bottoms; and he mentions that the anus of the little girl was so dilated that it was nearly confounded with her vagina.

These facts give us some idea of the enlargement of the anus that may arise from sodomy, and help to explain some of Martial's epigrams.

There have also been some interesting remarks privately published by a recent traveller through the realms of the King of Bokhara.

He speaks of that monarch having two wings to his harem, one for boys and one for girls. When the King would have connexion with one of his boys, the latter is well purged and brought to the King fasting, scents and oil being injected up his bottom. Then the boy has his dinner to give him courage and spirits to amuse the King, after which his Majesty has the boy in the presence generally of two or three of the royal wives. This traveller speaks of the salacious ways of these boys, the enlargement of their bottom-holes, and growths around the orifice, which made it appear very like the private parts of a woman.

Tardieu speaks of this growth too, but he also speaks of other developments, as well as the consequences of passive sodomy, such as piles and various disagreeable matters. We think, too, that the King of Bokhara's habit of purging his boys before having connexion with them corroborates Tardieu's statement and the observations of many others, that the effect of being continually buggered (and Tardieu suggests as well the use of laxative ointments), is to so relax the *sphincter ani* that it will not retain the faeces.

In the most civilized places of the present day sodomy with males is rarely practised—with females it is practised oftener; but in Rome it was the habit, the recognized habit, and it only became hateful when the man always received the attention and never gave. In those days men loved a lusty fellow as much as women do now, and the lusty fellow could give as much pleasure to a man as he could to a woman, and be thought none the worse for it.

The vice was so general and fashionable that the chastest of the Caesars, Augustus, was charged by many mouths with practising it; but Suetonius says, excepting his weakness for deflowering little girls, all the charges brought against him were calumnies.

Tiberius revelled in sodomy, and was surrounded by lusty Catamites, and rendered his name imperishable by indelibly connecting it with the Spintriae. At this chaste court Vitellus was apprenticed, and soon acquired the name of Spintria, raising his family by his prostitution, and showing when he in his time came to the throne, what a long train of evil one bad man in power can lay.

Caligula's mutual prostitutions with his pantomimic friend were well known, as was also his connexion with certain hostages; and the state of Roman decency may be presumed when we are told that V. Catullus, a young man of consular family, bawled out publicly that he had been having the Emperor until his back ached.

Claudius stuck to women; although he saw no harm in boys being debauched. Even his own son-in-law (to show the prevalence of the vice), we may observe, was stabbed and murdered while in the act of having his favourite boy.

Nero, of course, is not behindhand, and shows himself a true Roman Emperor by having the young Aulus Plautius by force, and then having him executed—the terrible result of worn-out desires, the irresistible impulse to remove from the face of the earth the man or woman you have satiated yourself with.

Our old friend Vitellus, when he came to the throne, managed the state entirely by the advice of the lowest classes, at the head of whom was the freedman Asiaticus, and his cabinet council was nothing but a series of mutual and unnatural pollutions.

Leaving Titus and the Eunuch, and Catamites, we will say one word on Galba, who bears the palm of Roman sodomites. He had no taste for women, nor had many a better man. He liked males, which was nothing uncommon; but he only fancied them when they were past their prime, and there he stood alone in his sodomy—he had not even the excuse of saying that the plump hips and smooth face of the boy resembled a girl. As another celebrated piece of royalty was fond of bad oysters, his taste was for old men—for men who had lived too long to enjoy pleasure or to give pleasure to anyone. But Galba, even when old Icelas brought the news of Nero's death, as he was sitting surrounded by friends, rose, kissed the old gentleman, and requesting him to make "a clear coast," led him into a private room, and had him. We can only say it would have been much more like Galba, if he had had the old gentleman there and then before all the company.

TRIBADISM

Dogging the heels of sodomy walks tribadism, a vice which every man in his heart looks on with kindly eyes. This sister vice appears to have existed from all ages. It is at least as old as sodomy, and still lives, aye, flourishes amongst the supposed modest maidens of our day. In all civilized Europe it exists among single women who have been debarred from men, generally in a narrowed sense, rarely taking other form than mutual frigging. But amongst some prostitutes of the upper class, and a few matrons of educated vicious tastes, it flourishes, the Frenchwomen bearing the palm. In the latter case gama-huching comes into free play; one woman loves another as jealously as ever a man could, and we have known instances in England of great unhappiness ensuing from one trib-ade giving up her inamorata for another man or woman; and in one memorable instance the forlorn one taking a revenge that very nearly involved the ruin of both.

The Count de Grammont mentions an instance in his memoirs of Miss Hobart, a maid of honour at the court of Charles the Second, being forbidden the royal presence for endeavouring to violate another maid of honour.

It is not clear how she was doing it, and it certainly is a mystery why that debauched monarch should have been so severe upon her.

No one can read Juvenal without being convinced that in Martial's time tribadism flourished in Rome. His de-scriptions of the feast of the Bona Dea leave no doubt of it.

If he did leave any doubt Martial clears it up by the pointedness of some of his epigrams. It flourished even to women with enlarged clitorises (hermaphrodites) having boys.

This is perfectly rational. Sodomy and tribadism go hand in hand. Where one reigns the other flourishes, and in their development they are nearly identical vices. Boys debarred from women frig themselves, frig each other, and then have each other, and are fortunate if they do not grow up to be sodomites. Girls debarred from men do the same with their own sex, and bloom into perfect tribades by a gamahuche.

This is one end of the stick; the other is as when a man, having plunged into all the possible debauchery with females, at last resorts to sodomy, or where a woman, say a prostitute of good position with many friends, gets satiated and tired when she has exhausted every letch of the male fancy; then she turns to her own sex for a new and piquant pleasure.

It is not long since we were sitting in a café in the Haymarket when a Frenchwoman of about thirty walked across the room to a young English girl and offered her ten shillings to be allowed to kiss her cunt.

THE END

Lightning Source UK Ltd.
Milton Keynes UK
UKOW01f2121300316

271217UK00001B/4/P